Scallywags

and the
Hungry Hairy
Sea Monster

BOOK 3

I'M HUNGRY!

Books by Cameron Stelzer

The Scallywags series:

Scallywags and the Troublesome Treasure
Scallywags and the Candy Catastrophe
Scallywags and the Hungry Hairy Sea Monster
Scallywags and the Stormy Secret

The Pie Rats series:

The Forgotten Map
The King's Key
The Island of Destiny
The Trophy of Champions
Child of the Cloud
The Golden Anchor

Drawing books:

How to Sketch Scallywags
How to Create Pie Rats
How to Draw Dragons
How to Create Cool Characters

The Stroogle series:

The Stroogle
The Stroogle's New Home
The Stroogle Warms Winter
The Stroogle Sails the Seven Seas
The Stroogle and the Golden Dragon
The Stroogle in Space

Scallywags
and the
Hungry Hairy
Sea Monster

BOOK 3

SCHOOL OF
SCALLYWAGS

SOS

MUCKING ABOUT   MAYHEM

MISCHIEF

Written and Illustrated by
Cameron Stelzer

DAYDREAM
PRESS

For Vaughn
Don't get scared! What you think is the Hungry Hairy Sea Monster is probably just an older brother. One of them is HUNGRY (though the other is not particularly HAIRY).

A huge thanks to Team Stelzer, Team Glover and all the students and teachers I worked with in 2017 and 2018. Your input has created a funnier, crazier story! C.S.

First published by Daydream Press, Brisbane, Australia, 2019
Text and illustrations copyright © Dr Cameron Stelzer 2019
Illustrations are graphite pencil on paper
Scallywags and the Hungry Hairy Sea Monster: Scallywags Book 3
ISBN: 978 0 6482804 2 2 (pbk.)

Printed in China by 1010 Printing International Limited

NATIONAL LIBRARY OF AUSTRALIA
A catalogue record for this book is available from the National Library of Australia

It's hungry and it's hairy,
and positively scary.
It pays to be quite wary
on any moonlit night.

Beware the hungry monster.
I swear it's no imposter!
And mind it does not chomp ya,
or give you one big fright!

So, if you hear a whistling,
or feel your whiskers bristling,
then don't be rash by risking
your safety.
Run!
Take flight!

BENNY BANANA PEEL
The Sea Shanty Gangster Rapper

Meet the Heroes

BUZZZZ

MISCHIEF & FLEAS

BREAKING NEWS!

SOS

SOS

Mischief McScruff
SEA DOG

Felicity 'Flick' Foulweather
CAT FISH

Plus some
Other Students

Samuel
So 'n' Slow
SLEEPY SAILOR

Nora
Nibblesworth
BUNNY BUCCANEER

STAR STUDENT

SOS

SOS

HOT CHIPS

The BIG Chipper

SOS

SALTY SEAGULL

Owen Undersea PIRATE (because he's got 8 legs)

Mischief's Got No Talent

I'm not what you'd call a **talented** kind of dog. Sure, I can fetch a stick and sniff out a buried bone. But when it comes to talent that's worthy of applause, I missed out big time.

I can't bark in tune.

I can't make things disappear in a **PUFF** of smoke (unless you're referring to my cooking).

And when it comes to acting, I'm about as wooden as a tree.

Worst of all, my doggy dancing, which I thought was rather COOL, has been described as *dodgy dancing*.

I can't juggle dog biscuits while balancing a half-chewed ball on my nose.

I can't chase my tail in a circle without collapsing in a dizzy heap on the ground.

And I only know one pirate joke:

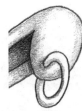

HOW MUCH DID THE BUNNY BUCCANEER PAY TO GET HER EARS PIERCED? HOW MUCH? A BUCK AN EAR!

On second thoughts, I can't even take credit for that joke. The school captain, Nora Nibblesworth, shared it with me while she was promoting the upcoming talent quest.

If one student at the School of Scallywags had a BUCKETLOAD of talent, it was Nora Nibblesworth.

Nora had a reputation for being the top of everything –

top speller,
top knotter,
top sailor,
top hopper.
The list goes on
and on
and on ...

SPELLING BEE
EISTEDDFOD
TSUNAMI ✓
ARCHIPELAGO ✓

It was hardly surprising that Nora's aunty gave her private tuition lessons after school, while I sat locked up in detention.

I'd lost track of how many times I'd been sent to the Dog House for Very Naughty Students to write out lines or to stare at a spot on the wall.

Believe me, it wasn't that I was a particularly naughty student. It was just that I was constantly being blamed for crimes that I didn't commit. The true crook at the School of Scallywags was Chomper O'Many.

Chomper was a saltwater crocodile with a **NASTY** habit of causing trouble, and an even **NASTIER** knack of getting away with it.

TROUBLE IS MY MIDDLE NAME!

Whenever Chomper committed a crime (which could happen on a Monday, a Tuesday, a Wednesday during PE, a Thursday afternoon, a Friday morning, a Saturday evening, and even on a Sunday) the headmaster automatically blamed me.

Take my latest detention, for instance. It was simply a case of being in the *wrong* place at the *wrong* time.

It all started when a marble statue of the school's first headmaster, Blacktail the Bold, was erected in the lilypond.

Thanks to an earlier catastrophe which destroyed Blacktail's famous black tail (again not my fault), Headmaster von Ironheart had decided to convert the statue into a fountain.

Where the tail had once been, now squirted a stream of dirty, black pondwater. It rose high into the air before *SPLASHING* down into the lilypond.

From a distance, the jet of water resembled a shaggy wolf's tail. It even swayed back and forth on windy days.

One morning, shortly after the statue had been erected, I was down by the pond, burying a couple of bones in Ye Olde School Garden, as all good Sea Dogs do.

I glanced up from my digging to see that the statue of Blacktail was no longer spraying water out of his †ail. He was spraying water out of his *nose!*

I'll spare you the juicy details, but I will say that Chomper must have **sneaked** into the SOS toilets during the night, **removed** a rusty metal pipe, **bent** it into the shape of an elephant's trunk, then **attached** it to the front of the statue.

Now I'm not usually one for kindergarten humour, but a ferocious wolf with an elephant's trunk was nothing short of hilarious. Even the headmaster's pet goldfish appeared to be laughing, blowing tiny bubbles to the surface of the water.

What I didn't find funny was that Headmaster von Ironheart chose that very moment to visit the lilypond with a jar of fish food under his arm.

I swear the goldfish began blowing bubbles at **me**.

The headmaster took one look at the statue's new trunk and put **TWO** and **TWO** together.

Unfortunately, he came up with *FIVE*.

It didn't help that I was grinning from ear to ear and covered in red garden soil, which the headmaster immediately mistook for rust.

I hurriedly tossed my bones into the radish patch and hoped I wasn't about to cop a *DOUBLE* detention for vegetable abuse.

'**A–HA!**' the headmaster exclaimed, grabbing my ear with a monstrous grizzly bear paw. 'I've caught you red-handed this time, Mischief McScruff! The guilt is written all over your face.'

'Oh n-n-no, sir, that's just dog slobber,' I stammered.

I wiped my mouth with the back of my paw, leaving a dirty, wet smear plastered across my face.

'Dribble, my foot!' Headmaster von Ironheart snorted. He pointed a finger at my cheek. 'That's pondwater right there. You've just earnt yourself a *TRIPLE* detention.'

I tried to explain that a pathetic pup with *minuscule* muscles lacked the strength to bend a metal pipe into an elephant's trunk. And, for a moment, the headmaster seemed to believe me.

Then he tossed me in the Dog House for Very Naughty Students, claiming that I must have hired a team of accomplices to do my dirty work.

And before I knew it, my three friends were hauled into the detention room and the door was *locked* behind us.

Mischief's Still Got No Talent

Hook Hand Horace and Benny Banana Peel were frequent visitors

to the Dog House for Very Naughty Students and they weren't surprised to find themselves invited to an all-day detention party.

DETENTION!
HOORAY!

Not that much PaRtYiNg ever took place in the Dog House.

Flick Foulweather looked far less relaxed about being dragged out of the art room to serve a triple detention for a crime she hadn't committed, or even heard of.

In fact, the black-furred cat looked ready to skin a rat as she entered the detention room. Not a pleasant thought if you happened to be Horace.

SCREEEEECH!

YIKES !!!

I glanced up at the barred windows hoping to see a beautiful blue sky overhead. Menacing **BLACK** storm clouds gathered in the sky.

Never a good sign when Flick is around, I thought with a gulp.

Flick suffered from **Foul Weather Syndrome**, an unfortunate condition that made her extremely grumpy on rainy days.

She was bearable if she had a paintbrush in her paws, but the Dog House was a place of punishment, not an art studio. Taking one look at her scowling face, I let her skulk off to the corner for a catnap before she considered skinning a **dog** instead of a **rat**.

Benny and Horace were a little more curious about the reason for our detention.

'So, tell me, Mischief,' Benny said in his thick jungle accent, 'what have we been accused of doing this time?'

'Vandalising school property,' I said vaguely.

'Rotten pies to school property,' Horace groaned. He used his hook to haul his tiny rat body onto his chair, scratching the wood in the process.

'That's the third time we've been charged with vandalism-related offences this week. Chomper must be running out of imagination.'

'If anything, Chomper is getting more **creative** with his pranks,' I said, recalling what I'd seen in the lilypond.

Benny put his feet up on a desk and slouched back in his chair. 'It must be the Shark Tooth Talent Quest. It's got the creative juices flowing.'

'I've heard that every SOS student is expected to enter,' Horace said. He raised his voice so that the old bloodhound at the front of the room could hear him. 'Apparently it counts towards our **REPORT CARDS.**'

Old Fetch lowered the horror book he was reading and stared blankly at Horace.

'Right you are, my lad,' he said in his GLOOMY voice. 'Although I doubt there are half-a-dozen students in this entire school worth watching on stage.'

'Well, Benny is one of them,' Horace said, thrusting his hook in the Chimp-at-Sea's direction (and almost impaling one of Benny's toes). 'He's a true entertainer. Aren't you, Benny?'

'Sure, Horace,' Benny said, sliding his feet off the desk.

ENTERTAINER IS MY MIDDLE NAME!

Horace scratched his head. 'I thought your middle name was **BANANA.** As in Benny **BANANA** Peel.'

Benny ignored him and went on to explain, 'We're putting together a group entry for the talent quest, Mischief. It's a history of Shark Tooth Island presented in a sea shanty gangster style. It starts with the shipwrecking of Blacktail's mighty galleon, the *Howling Queen*, and ends with the legend of the Hungry Hairy Sea Monster.'

Old Fetch let out a loud snort. 'The Hungry Hairy Sea Monster is no legend, my lad. It's as **real** as I am!'

'That doesn't say much,' Horace muttered. 'Half the students think you're a *GHOST.*'

'I can assure you I'm very much alive and well,' Old Fetch moaned in a voice that sounded positively *GHASTLY.* 'And I intend to remain that way by staying well clear of that Bog.'

He pointed a stumpy finger at a wall map of Shark Tooth Island and lowered his voice to a whisper. 'They say that on moonlit nights the Hungry Hairy Sea Monster roams the

Bog in search of its next meal. If you listen carefully from the library windows, you might even hear the wind whistling through the creature's long hair.'

whhhhhhhhhhh...

'It's a good thing we don't hang around the library at midnight,' Benny said.

'Or the Bog,' I added with a gulp.

'Rotten pies to crazy superstitions,' Horace scoffed. 'There's nothing to be afraid of in the Bog – except the sewage pipe from the SOS toilets. Trust me, you do **NOT** want to see what comes out of there!'

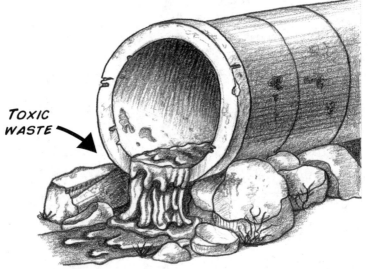

TOXIC WASTE

Superstition or not, the Hungry Hairy Sea Monster was not a creature I wanted to *hear*, see, or be **eaten** by. I vowed to remain tucked up in bed whenever the

moon was out.

Returning my attention to the problem at hand, I whispered to Benny, 'Any chance you could use a **THIRD** member in your group? The talent quest is tomorrow night and I haven't organised an act.'

Horace gestured to the sleeping cat. 'We already have a third member. Flick is in charge of lighting and costumes.'

'And she's painting us a backdrop,' Benny added.

Flick raised her head and moaned. 'I *was* painting you a backdrop until the headmaster took away my paints and threw me in the Dog House.'

'Yeah, sorry about that,' I muttered. 'What about a **FOURTH** member?'

'Err, we already have one of those, too,' Horace said awkwardly. 'Sir Squawk-a-lot offered to be our stuntman and special effects technician. Nothing flash, mind you. Just flying across the stage, setting off the odd **EXPLOSION**. He's popping around this evening for a costume fitting.'

'Oh,' I said, unable to hide my disappointment. 'Well, good luck to you and your toucan.'

'Hang on,' Benny said, thoughtfully. 'It wouldn't hurt to have a **FIFTH** member in our group if we seriously want to win the competition. From all reports, Nora Nibblesworth has put together a magnificent

act and Chomper has almost perfected his knife throwing routine.'

'**Ouch,**' Horace winced.

Benny raised his fake eyepatch and studied me closely. 'What special talents do you possess, Mischief?'

'Um, well ... err, nothing immediately springs to mind,' I said, scratching my chin.

'You're good at sniffing out trouble,' Horace offered.

'As well as getting *INTO* trouble,' Flick added from across the room. 'Though I hardly think trouble-making is classed as a talent.'

'Can you play any musical instruments?' Benny asked. 'Horace has the percussion section covered, but we could do with a banjo or a bugle to spice things up.'

HONK!

'Hmm, my Uncle Mutthew did teach me a few tunes on the fiddle,' I said. 'Some of the classics like,

SHE'LL BE COMIN' 'ROUND THE HEADLAND,
THERE'S A HOLE IN MY ROWBOAT,
and everyone's favourite,
WHAT SHALL WE DO WITH THE FLEA-RIDDEN SEA DOG?
But I'd hardly say my fiddling is at an orchestral standard.'

'Bah, rotten pies to orchestral standards!' Horace scoffed. 'Sea shanty gangster raps aren't about perfection. They're about passion.'

'Yeah, and *Passion* is my middle name,' Benny said. He thumped his hairy chest, setting his gangster chains jingling.

'You certainly have a lot of middle names, Benny,' Horace remarked.

'So, what do you say, Mischief?' Benny asked. 'Are you *in* or are you *in?*'

'I guess I'm *in,*' I said. 'Sign me up for a dose of sea shanty fiddling!'

'You do have a fiddle, don't you, Mischief?' Flick asked suspiciously.

'Err … not exactly,' I confessed. I reached into my pocket and pulled out a pawful of loose change. 'But I DO have some birthday money from my Uncle Mutthew and I've heard there's a music shop in Port Scoundrel.'

'Is there ever!' Horace said excitedly. He scraped his hook against the desktop, creating even more damage to school property. 'Madam Melody's Marvellous Music Shop is the SECOND coolest shop in the port – after Pandora's Pie Palace.

I mean, where else can you buy a drum-stick attachment for a hook hand at fifty percent off the recommended retail price?'

Benny raised a ringed finger into the air. 'I wouldn't know, Horace. I've never needed one.'

Horace shot Flick a sideways glance. 'Well, I wouldn't need one either if a crummy Cat Fish hadn't bitten off my paw and left me several fingers down.'

'Hey, don't look at me like that,' Flick snapped. 'I'm a fishatarian!'

'Then it's fortunate that I'm not a fish,' Horace muttered. 'Otherwise I would have **ZERO** fingers left.'

GULP!

'What kind of argument is that?' Flick said. 'Fish don't have fingers. They have fins.'

'So, how do you explain *fish fingers* then?' Horace said triumphantly.

'Err, perhaps we should get started on our performance,' I interrupted. 'Unless you'd prefer to spend the next six hours discussing each other's dietary preferences.'

'Mmm, bananas,' Benny said, licking his lips. 'I could talk about bananas all day long …'

A Rather Peculiar Shopping List

Fortunately, Benny didn't spend the next six hours talking about bananas. He did, however, try to rhyme *Howling Queen* with **bananas are green.**

We convinced him to use **the sea is green** instead.

By the time our triple detention was over, Benny had almost completed his sea shanty gangster rap and Old Fetch was staring at us in disgust.

'I admit, the ending needs a little work,' Benny said as we were *BOOTED* out of the Dog House. 'But with some first-class fiddling and a couple of stage props, the audience is gonna love it!'

I didn't have the heart to tell him that we'd need more than a few papier-mâché trees and an upbeat pirate jig to beat Nora Nibblesworth. What we needed was a dramatic finale – something that truly

brought the legend of the Hungry Hairy Sea Monster to life. But what that something was, I really *didn't* know.

Horace offered to accompany me to Port Scoundrel to purchase my fiddle, with the excuse that he needed a tambourine attachment for his hook hand. I suspected he was more interested in visiting Pandora's Pie Palace for happy hour.

The small flyer tucked into his belt read:

For all-you-can-eat pies, visit

PANDORA'S  PIE PALACE

where every pie* comes with a smile
(oh, and free sauce)

Happy Hour is 5pm to 6pm

*Gluten-free, dairy-free, sugar-free, nut-free,
preservative-free, low carb, low fat, low GI,
salt-reduced, vitamin-enriched, high fibre,
vegan, vegetarian, paleo, fishatarian options are
available (plus all your unhealthy favourites)

**PANDORA'S PIE PALACE IS THE PROUD
SPONSOR OF THE SOS PIE DRIVE**

Putting in her order for a fishatarian pie (no sauce), Flick headed back to the art room to continue working on her backdrop. Luckily the storm had passed, and she was back to her normal only-slightly-moody self.

Meanwhile, Benny went in search of a full-length mirror to practice his:

> ULTRA-COOL,
> ULTRA-HIP,
> ULTRA-SNAZZY
> GANGSTER RAP
> MOVES!

His words, not mine.

With Horace by my side, I began the STEEP climb up the flying fox tower. The only way to reach Port Scoundrel from the School of Scallywags (without squelching through the Bog) was to take the flying fox.

Horace and I reached the top of the spiral staircase to find Samuel So 'n' Slow manning the flying fox winch.

'Afternoon, Sam,' Horace said cheerfully to the sleepy sloth.

'Good … after … noon … Hook … Hand … Horace,' Samuel replied in his slow-as-a-sloth's voice. Then, turning to me, he added, 'Good … after … noon … Mischief … Mc … Scruff … What … can … I … do … for … you … today?'

FIVE minutes later, when he had finally finished his question, I replied, 'Hi Samuel, we're heading down to the port. Do you want anything from the shops?'

Samuel's eyes lit up like a dawn sky –
slowly, ever so slowly.

'I … need … a … costume … for … my … interpretive … dance … performance,' he said. Reaching down, he removed a small coin bag from his belt – which took another *FIVE MINUTES*.

'We're not exactly experts when it comes to dance costumes,' I confessed as he tipped several coins into my paw. 'But we'll try our best to fix you up with something InTerPREtiVe.'

'Thank … you … so … much … Misch –' Samuel began, but Horace cut him off.

'Yes, yes, you're eternally grateful and all that nonsense. We get the picture.' Horace plonked himself down on the seat and gestured for me to join him. 'Now, if we could just get a move on before the shops shut, and HAPPY hour turns to HUNGRY hour …'

Samuel pointed to a list of rules on the wall. 'One … at … a … time,' he said slowly.

'Rotten pies to one at a time!' Horace snapped in frustration. 'If it's the weight you're worried about, then don't. Mischief is scrawnier than an underfed budgerigar and I weigh less than one of Chomper's toes.'

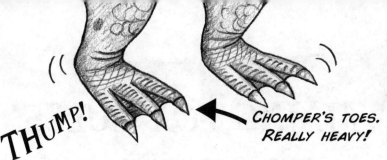

THUMP!

(( ))

CHOMPER'S TOES.
REALLY HEAVY!

I looked down at my underdeveloped biceps and made a mental note to visit the SOS gym. Then I remembered the gym had been converted into a **TORTURE** chamber and hurriedly dismissed the idea.

In front of me, Horace was still arguing with Samuel So 'n' Slow.

'… and technically six Mischiefs carrying bone-filled backpacks would still be lighter than one Chomper O'Many.'

'Single … passengers … only,' Samuel said, refusing to budge. 'Head … master's … orders.'

I ran my eye over the list of rules. It was a long list. Sure enough, there was the *single riders only* rule right at the top. I tried to recall how many *other* rules Horace had broken during his time at the School of Scallywags.

Was it seven? Or more like seventy …?

FLYING FOX RULES

Single riders only.

No standing on the flying fox.

No dancing on the flying fox.

No tightrope walking on the flying fox.

No juggling pointy objects
while tightrope walking on the
flying fox (unless you are a
qualified circus performer).

No eating spicy Mexican
food on the flying fox.

No letting off wind after eating
spicy Mexican food on the flying
fox. The Bog stinks enough as it is!

Do not exceed the speed limit
of 587.3 km per hour.

No throwing school books into the Bog.

No throwing report cards into the Bog. Be proud of your failures!

No throwing miniature matchstick model ships into the Bog. They will break.

No throwing hopes and dreams into the Bog. Especially if you hope to join a famous boy band. That dream will never come true.

No yelling WHEEEE or YIPEEE or GERONIMO after 8pm at night. Young children are trying to sleep.

The punishment for breaking any rule is to clean the SOS toilets for a month. And you do NOT want to know what's in there!

BY ORDER OF
Headmaster von Ironheart

Horace opened his mouth to make another one of his rotten-pie remarks, but I jumped in with, 'It's okay, Samuel. You can send Horace down first. I can wait.'

'Are you sure?' Horace asked, looking slightly guilty. 'This was supposed to be *your* shopping trip.'

'I'm positive,' I said with a dismissive wave of my paw. 'I won't need long to pick out a fiddle and the Uni-Corn Shop for Fashion, Magic Tricks and Fresh Vegetables is sure to have a dance costume in Samuel's size.'

'Or a lettuce tutu he can wear,' Horace scoffed. 'Whoever heard of a shop that sells clothing, corn on the cob and card tricks under the same roof?'

I shrugged. 'It's the way of the future. Look, why don't you get started at the Pie Palace? I'll meet you there when I'm done.'

'If you insist,' Horace said. He gave me a small salute with his hook, almost poking out his eye.

'Have … a … nice … ride … Horace …' Samuel said, pulling the release leaver.

Horace barely had time to find a hook hold before he was rocketing down the cable at 587.4 km per hour (and breaking yet another rule).

'Don't forget my tambourine attachment!' he shouted back. 'I'll save a bone pie for *yoooouu u u u ..*' His voice was swept away in the wind.

Thirty minutes later, after Samuel So 'n' Slow had winched the flying fox back up to the tower, I was enjoying my own ride down to the port. If you could call a daredevil ride with no safety harness *ENJOYABLE.*

Beneath me lay the Bog in all of its gruesome glory – a marshy, muddy wasteland where no pirate dared to tread. Through wispy patches of mist, I could just make out the shapes of **SHADOWY BLACK** shrubs and pools of stagnant water dotting the landscape. Stringy clumps of seaweed, washed up during high tides, lay rotting in the late afternoon sunlight.

Even from a great height, I could smell the foul aroma of the place. Horace wasn't kidding about that SOS sewage pipe.

Before I knew it, the mist had vanished, and the buildings of Port Scoundrel were rising around me.

If I could improve one thing about the flying fox (apart from the unpleasant scenery, the terrible smell and the lack of safety equipment), it would be the dismount.

Reaching the clocktower in the centre of the port, the flying fox came to a sudden, jarring halt, sending me *flying* out of my seat. I somersaulted through the air and landed nose-first in a huge pile of straw.

The fancy sign above the straw read *ARRIVALS LOUNGE.* I thought a more appropriate description would be:

After checking that I hadn't been pickpocketed by any of the street mice that lived in the straw, I set off in the direction of Madam Melody's shop, leaving a trail of straw behind me.

Fashion 'n' Stuff

Madam Melody's Marvellous Music Shop was situated in a rundown part of the port. Not that you could tell the difference between the rundown part of the port and the rest of the port. Half the buildings I passed needed a new coat of paint. The other half needed **NEW WALLS, NEW WINDOWS, NEW DOORS,** and *then* a **NEW COAT OF PAINT!**

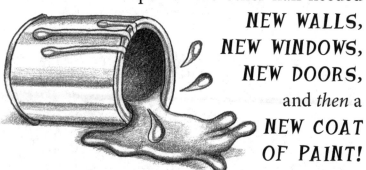

I guessed a bit of wear and tear was to be expected in a town run by scoundrels and gangsters.

It was almost half past five when I turned into Scat Alley and began walking towards Madam Melody's store.

Several doors from my destination, I stopped at the entrance to the Uni-Corn Shop for Fashion, Magic Tricks and Fresh Vegetables (a rather long-winded name for a department store).

Through the open window, I saw the shop's owner, Miss Sparkle, filling a hat-shaped box with playing cards, silk scarves and bright-orange carrots.

Miss Sparkle claimed to be a real-life unicorn, but everyone knew she was just a *pony* with a *corncob* stuck to her head.

'Greetings to you on this most magical evening,' she said in a magical, sparkly voice.

'Oh, hi there,' I replied in a voice that was neither **magical** nor **sparkly**.

She looked me up and down for a moment.

'Are you hunting for a *SNAZZY* new suit, or perhaps you would like to try some of my famous fresh corn?' she said.

'Err, I'm just after a dance costume, Miss Sparkle,' I said awkwardly. 'It's for a friend.'

'Of course it is,' she said with a wink. She pointed a hoof towards the stairs. 'Dance costumes are on the first floor, between the magic wands and the celery aisle. Oh, and the *SNAZZY* new suits are a little further along.'

Trying to hide my reddening cheeks, I dashed towards the stairs. Spotting my reflection in a full-length mirror, I realised

that a **SNAZZY** new suit wasn't such a bad idea after all. I certainly wasn't the picture of high-fashion with my crumpled newspaper hat and straw-covered school blazer. Then I realised that I didn't have the money for a **SNAZZY** new suit, let alone a tatty old one.

The scarecrow look will have to do, I told myself.

I found the dance costume section overflowing with leotards, unitards, tutus, feather boas and other pretty dance accessories. Unfortunately, the colour selection was limited to shades of pink.

'I hope Samuel likes pink,' I muttered.

I chose a pink leotard with flowing pink tassels and a matching pink tutu.

After paying for Samuel's dance outfit (which Miss Sparkle placed in a pretty pink carry bag), I continued down Scat Alley. I was surprised to see an enormously wide hippo standing in the doorway to the music shop. She wore a sleeveless dress, which revealed a line of music note tattoos on each arm.

I recognised the tune on her left arm as:

♩ **Simple Simon met a pieman** ♫
going to the fair.

The tune on her right arm looked suspiciously like another pie-related rhyme:

Sing a song of sixpence,
a pocket full of rye, four
and twenty blackbirds
♫ **baked in a pie.** ♩♪

Yet another two lines of music note tattoos were visible on the hippo's legs. There was no mistaking the tunes:

Little Jack Horner sat in a corner, eating his Christmas pie,

and

Georgie Porgie, pudding and pie, kissed the girls and made them cry.

Clearly Horace wasn't the only one on the island who loved pies.

The hippo reached for the shop's **OPEN** sign and was just about to flip it to **CLOSED** when I arrived at her doorstep.

She took one look at me, covered in straw and looking like a scarecrow, and let out a *GASP* of surprise.

I was almost blown off my feet by a blast of pie-scented breath.

Her open mouth was enormous, easily as big as my head and, for a moment, I feared she would swallow me **WHOLE**.

Then she gathered her nerves, put her hand on her chest and burst into song.

> ♪ Blessed Mozart, take a look!
> A scarecrow at my door.
> Whatever shall I do, my dear?
> I'm terrified of straw! ♫

Before I had time to explain that I wasn't, in fact, a real scarecrow and that the straw was one-hundred-percent organic, Madam Melody had already launched into a second verse of her opera.

> ♪ Now, don't be silly,
> dear old girl.
> A match should do the trick.

A scarecrow burns like
autumn leaves.
It's easy, fun and quick.

'It's not fun if you're the poor scarecrow,'
I said, removing a few strands of straw from
my newspaper hat.

Madam Melody was too
wrapped up in her performance to hear me.

I must confess,
I don't have time
to roast that poor young lad.
I'd miss the end of happy hour,
and wouldn't that be sad?

Oh yes, my dear,
a pie-less night
would be an awful shame.
And if you burnt down
half the shop,
you'd have yourself to blame.

It's settled then.
I'll do what's right
and ask the poor chap in.
Perhaps he wants to buy a horn,
a flute or violin.

Err, Melody, it seems that while
you've chatted here outside,
that scruffy-looking scarecrow
has already crept inside!

Crawling through the hippo's legs, I entered the cluttered shop.

I stared around in wonder. The place was a musician's paradise.

Every inch of the shop was covered with instruments. Horns and harps, harmonicas and harpsichords were piled from the floor to the ceiling. There were violins and violas, pianos and piccolos and an assortment of colourful lutes. Some were **NEW.** Some were **OLD.** Some were downright **ANCIENT!**

72

After staggering around in a musical daze, I eventually located the hook hand instrument section near the rear of the store. Sure enough, most of the items were on sale for *FIFTY PERCENT OFF*.

I guess there aren't too many one-pawed musicians in Port Scoundrel, I thought.

I selected a jingly tambourine attachment for Horace and then made my way to the strings' section.

I was excited to discover an entire wall of fiddles. I was far less excited to learn what they cost.

I **GULPED** as I read the first price tag. The battered old fiddle was way out of my price range. And it was one of the cheapies.

Madam Melody, having overcome her fear of straw, hesitantly approached me as I browsed a row of fiddles on a shelf marked:

TO BE REPAIRED

'Do you have anything a little less expensive?' I asked politely.

'Hmm,' Madam Melody considered. 'Maybe I do ...'

She shuffled over to the *Antiques* section and picked up an old wooden case. Turning to face me, she launched into song:

♪ For a reasonable price
I have something that's nice.
It's a fiddle of
legend and fame.
If you play it at night,
under twinkling starlight,
you'll enchant all the
maidens and dames! ♪♪

She opened the case to reveal a small brown fiddle and a matching bow. The fiddle was in sound condition, though there didn't appear to be anything **enchanting** about it.

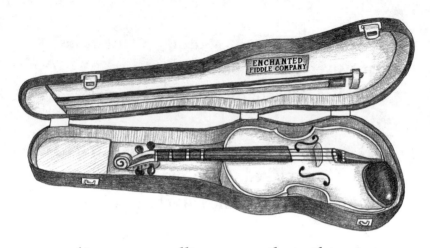

'Are you telling me that this is a ☆**magical**☆ fiddle?' I asked. 'Like in those fairy tales, where the hero puts a fire-breathing dragon to sleep by playing a soothing tune?'

Madam Melody looked away guiltily.

'Err, not exactly,' she said in a far less operatic voice. 'But they do say that every musical instrument contains a TINY spark of ☆**magic**.'☆

'Hmm,' I said, glancing at the price tag. 'Magic or no magic, this is the only fiddle I can afford. I'll **TAKE** it.'

Pie and Chips

I left the shop clutching the fiddle case under one arm and my pretty pink carry bag under the other.

Madam Melody had graciously thrown in a free triangle attachment for Horace. I also received a complimentary copy of *Fiddlers' Weekly*, which contained some well-known fiddling tunes such as **Hey Diddle Diddle, the Cat and the Fiddle,** plus songs from the hit pirate musical **Fiddler on the Poop Deck.**

When I mentioned that I was heading to

Pandora's Pie Palace for happy hour, Madam Melody offered to walk with me.

'I'm meeting some friends in the **VIP** Room,' she explained. 'The *Very Important Pies* Room.'

After Madam Melody had locked, re-locked, deadlocked, padlocked, bolted and chained the front door, we made our way towards the Pie Palace.

Walking down the grimy sidewalk, we chatted casually about celebrity fiddlers, the SOS pie drive, and my Uncle Mutthew's four failed attempts to win **Doggy's Got Talent.**

It wasn't long before Madam Melody let slip that she was one of three judges for the Shark Tooth Talent Quest. By the time we

had reached the Pie Palace I knew the names of the other two judges: Headmaster von Ironheart and Legs Lorraine.

Legs Lorraine was a spotted French frog with extremely long legs who taught plank diving at the Muddy Puddle Swim School. She was also a former international swimwear model who wore nothing but string bikinis.

OOOH LA LA!

Benny once told me that her middle name was *FASHION*. Horace had insisted that she had two middle names: *FASHION* and *DISASTER*. Being a bit of a fashion disaster myself (dare I mention the scarecrow incident) I had wisely stayed out of the argument.

As I stood outside Pandora's Pie Palace, considering the three judges and their areas of expertise, I realised that my slim chance of winning the talent quest was now SKELETALLY slim.

With Headmaster von Ironheart, Legs Lorraine and Madam Melody on the judging panel, only an *Einstein* in a *pop diva's* body would ever stand a chance. Not only would the champion act have to be musically brilliant, it would also have to be super-stylish and packed with educational content.

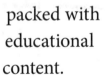

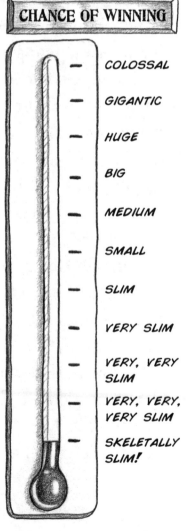

CHANCE OF WINNING

- COLOSSAL
- GIGANTIC
- HUGE
- BIG
- MEDIUM
- SMALL
- SLIM
- VERY SLIM
- VERY, VERY SLIM
- VERY, VERY, VERY SLIM
- SKELETALLY SLIM!

I knew there was only one act that fit that description, and it was *not* our sea shanty gangster rap.

It was **Nora the Magnificent.**

Nora the Magnificent was Nora Nibblesworth's stage name. Her act consisted of *Nora* performing *magnificent* feats on stage. It wasn't the most creative of stage names, but it certainly was catchy.

Everyone at school knew about Nora the Magnificent. In fact, everyone on the island had heard of her. She was the face of the talent quest – the drawcard of the event. Without her the ticket sales would be woeful and the talent would be even worse.

The freshly-printed poster plastered to a nearby lamp post said it all:

COME AND SEE
NORA THE
MAGNIFICENT

Performing at the Shark Tooth Talent Quest

BE
AMAZED

BE
MYSTIFIED

ONE NIGHT ONLY – SATURDAY 7 PM

ALSO APPEARING:
Fashion by Deluchio
The Salty Seagulls Community Choir
Wendi the Hilarious Hyena
Samuel's Interpretive Dance Studio
Chomper and his Nasty Knives
The Sea Shanty Gangster Rapper*
Plus some other random SOS acts

*Warning: The Sea Shanty Gangster Rap may contain
toilet humour, dodgy rhymes and references to rotten
bananas. It is recommended for immature audiences only.

Oh great, I thought, reading the warning message at the bottom of the poster. *If that's not an invitation to throw rotten tomatoes at our act, I don't know what is.*

The thought had barely crossed my mind, when a slice of piping-hot ᴛomaᴛo pie came whizzing through the open window of Pandora's Pie Palace, missing my head by millimetres.

'**BLIMEY!**' I exclaimed, ducking for cover behind Madam Melody. 'We're under attack!'

I watched in shock as the flying pie splattered into the talent quest poster, staining the portrait of Nora red and spraying chunks of steaming tomatoes in every direction.

'Soggy salad vegetables!' I gulped. 'It's a tough job being an entertainer. I haven't even taken to the stage and the critics are taking pot shots at me!'

Madam Melody didn't seem the least bit concerned about the attack. But, as an experienced performer, she was used to having the odd rotten tomato (or tomato pie) thrown in her direction.

Leaving Madam Melody at the entrance to the **VIP** Room (which was a scarecrow-free zone), I strapped the fiddle to my back and began commando-crawling through the bustling heart of Pandora's Pie Palace.

Glancing up at the pie-shaped tables, it wasn't hard to spot my attacker. Although *attacker* is probably not the best way to describe a **PINT−SIZED** Pie Rat having the time of his life.

Horace was standing on the top of a table, surrounded by a flock of Salty Seagulls. They were led by The Big Chipper, SOS's reigning chip-eating champion.

Not surprisingly, the seagulls were gulping down hot chips from *Pandora's Pie and Chips Party Boxes,* while Horace polished off the pies and gave the seagulls something to squawk about.

The stumpy rat was singing, dancing and flapping his arms around like a chorus girl in a cabaret show.

Every now and then, his wayward hook would clip the edge of a pie, sending pastry and pie filling hurtling through the front window.

The seagulls were loving it. They SQUAWKED and SCREECHED and SHOOK their tailfeathers in delight as Horace belted out his favourite sea shanties.

He didn't have Benny's style or Madam Melody's pitch, but what he lacked in skill he more than made up for in passion.

It's a Pie Rat's life for me and that means pies for tea. I'll fill my tum with apple pie and sometimes strawberry.

 PIES!

♫. It's a Pie Rat's life for me
as you can plainly see.
I've eaten pies on mountain tops
and munched them up a tree.

PIES!

It's a Pie Rat's life for me,
but I've got enemies.
Pursued by nasty crocodiles
across the seven seas. ♫

Shh!

Horace lowered his voice to a whisper,
changing the tune for the next verse.

♪ But if the pies go rotten
in the middle of the night,
I'll load them in a cannon
and give Chomper such a fright! ♪

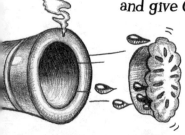

BOOM!

The Salty Seagulls roared with laughter, sending chip crumbs and stray feathers flying into the air.

Horace doubled his volume for the final verse.

IT'S A PIE RAT'S LIFE FOR ME,
THE ONLY LIFE FOR ME.
AND PIES ARE WHAT I'M ALL ABOUT,
SO SING ALONG WITH MEEEEEEEEE!

In a flash, The Big Chipper had joined Horace with his own version of the shanty.

It's a seagull's life for me,
and I like chips for tea,
with lots of sauce and vinegar
and salt straight from the sea.

CHIPS!

The Big Chipper continued his ode to deep-fried potato chips, but my attention was drawn to a large reptilian figure rising from the shadows in a dark corner of the room. The steam rising from his nose told me that he was **NOT** enjoying the evening's entertainment.

'Soggy dog biscuits!' I gasped. 'What's Chomper O'Many doing here?'

My first answer to this question was *eating pies*, quickly followed by *about to eat Horace*.

Without giving it a third thought, I dragged myself off the ground and went bounding over to the seagulls' table.

Horace clearly hadn't noticed the giant saltwater crocodile thundering towards him, and he was still singing away happily with The Big Chipper, while stuffing his face with pies.

Hot chips and pies, we'll eat them all our lives.

'Quick,' I yelled, grabbing Horace by the hook. 'We have to leave!'

'Already?' Horace said with an enormous burp. 'But I haven't had dessert!'

'You **are** dessert!' I hissed. 'Come on, before Chomper asks for a rat's tail waffle cone with a scoop of dog sorbet.'

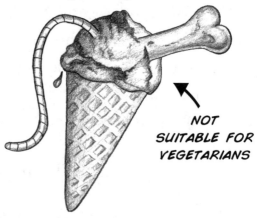

NOT SUITABLE FOR VEGETARIANS

Horace glanced around frantically.

'Chomper!' he exclaimed. 'Chomper O'Many is here for **happy** hour?'

'Yeah,' I said, dragging Horace through the flock of seagulls. 'And unless we find a back door fast, happy hour is about to become our **final** hour.'

Dark Alleyways

We **BARGED** through the crowded Pie Palace in our frantic bid to escape. The place was a maze of pie carts and sauce stations. It was a struggle not to trip on a chair leg or faceplant into a barrel of whipped cream. I would have stopped to admire Pandora's famous *Leaning Tower of Pies* if there had not been a two-tonne croc snapping at my heels.

THE LEANING TOWER OF PIES
BETTER THAN THE LEANING TOWER OF PIZZA

Behind us, Chomper had reached the seagulls' table and, with a sweep of his tail, sent party boxes and partying birds flying through the air.

I darted around a cutlery trolley, spotting a sign reading:

BACK DOOR STAFF ONLY
(and anyone being chased by an angry crocodile)

'This way!' I hissed.

Seeing safety in sight, Horace stopped at a serving cart to snatch up a couple of pies. He thrust one under each arm, muttering, 'One for Flick and one for the road.'

I was surprised the guy could think about pies at such a time, but then he was a **PIE** Rat.

We reached the back door to hear cutlery clattering to the ground behind us. I didn't

look back, but I guessed that Chomper had decided to go *STRAIGHT THROUGH* the cutlery trolley.

I grabbed the door handle and gave it a firm twist.

For once, luck was on my side, and the handle turned easily in my paw.

With Horace beside me, I threw the door open and leapt into the narrow alleyway.

We had only gone a couple of paces when a shadowy figure stepped out from behind a garbage bin, **BLOCKING** our path to safety.

'Whoa,' I gasped, skidding to a halt.

Horace was a little slower to react. He ploughed straight into the figure, losing his grip on the pies. One of the pies landed upside down on the pavement, the other one landed *upside down* on Horace's head.

'Hey, watch it,' the figure snapped, pushing Horace roughly away. 'You'll leave pie stains on my *SNAZZY* new suit.'

95

A second figure stepped out from behind the bin and let out an ear-splitting cackle. 'Ha, ha, ha.'

'Uh oh,' Horace gulped as sticky pie filling began oozing down the side of his face. 'I know that laugh.'

I knew the laugh, too – and it didn't make me feel all warm and fuzzy inside. In fact, it made me feel like sticking a piece of bubble gum in each ear and then burying my head in a bucket of sand.

I watched as a spotted hyena crept out of the shadows to join her companion in the centre of the alleyway. The handsome grey wolf was clearly wearing one of Miss Sparkle's *SNAZZY* new suits. I had to admit, it looked pretty *SNAZZY* on him.

The hyena didn't look quite as *SNAZZY*. She raised her paw and pointed to a line of berry juice running down Horace's cheek.

'You've just reminded me of a really funny joke,' she announced with a chuckle.

Horace groaned, 'Wendi Whiptongue and Deluchio da Silva. Trust you two scumbags to be hiding in a dingy alley.'

'Oh, we weren't hiding,' Wendi cackled. 'We were merely waiting to see who came through that door.'

'Well, here we are,' Horace said. 'Two innocent pie lovers in search of a *TOILET*. Nothing of interest. Now, if you'd kindly let us pass, we have places to be and bladders to empty.'

He tried to push past them, but they held their ground and refused to let him pass.

'You're not going anywhere,' Deluchio said with a voice as smooth as silk.

'Why not?' I asked, putting on my toughest voice, which made me sound like a deflating balloon. 'It's a free alleyway.'

'Not for nasty name callers, it's not,' Wendi snapped.

Horace gave me a sideways glance. 'N-n-name callers? That doesn't sound like us.'

'I beg to differ,' Deluchio said. 'A little birdy told us that someone has been bad-mouthing our dear friend, Chomper O'Many, in a particularly nasty song.'

'**SEVEN** nasty songs, to be precise,' Wendi cut in.

'Oh,' Horace gulped. 'You heard them **ALL?**'

'Aye,' Wendi spat. 'Especially the line:

'Chomper's homemade pies aren't fit for dirty flies.'

'F-fancy that,' Horace spluttered. 'And here I was thinking that Chomper was a world-class chef.'

Deluchio eyed us coolly. 'We figured the guilty party would try to make a sneaky exit out the back door.'

'The back door?' Horace laughed weakly.

'Don't be ridiculous. This isn't a cheesy detective novel. No one in their right mind escapes out the **BACK** door. They escape through the **FRONT** door.' Horace gestured in the direction of the main entrance. 'I'm certain I saw your guilty party fleeing just now. **Plump** fellow. Lots of feathers. Short beak. Terrible singer … yes, it was definitely him. You can still catch him if you hurry –'

Horace was interrupted by a gravelly voice from the doorway. 'Well, well, well. If it isn't my two least favourite classmates trapped in a dark and secluded alley. How very fortunate for me.'

CHEESY READING

I spun around to see Chomper O'Many stepping into the alley. His evil eyes glinted in the twilight. Several knives and forks were sticking out from between the folds of his scaly skin, but he hadn't noticed them.

'Psst,' Horace whispered. 'By *least favourite classmates* do you think Chomper is referring to **US** or Mr **SNAZZY** suit and the Heckling Hyena?'

'I'm pretty certain he's referring to **US**,' I said as the enormous crocodile lumbered closer.

'Rotten pies to **US**,' Horace moped. 'Whoever said *life wasn't a popularity contest,* clearly never found themselves trapped in a dark and secluded alley with three thugs and a drooling dog.'

'Hey, steady on,' I said, wiping drool from my chin. 'We're in this together.'

'Oh, you're in this together, all right,' Chomper spat. He ripped the lid off a garbage bin, flooding the alley with a repulsive, rotten stench. 'You're up to your necks in it!'

And before I had time to say or do anything, Chomper had grabbed me by the scruff of my neck and was lifting me off my feet.

'Looks like it's time to take out the trash!' Wendi cackled.

Horace tried to dart away, but Chomper scooped him up with his free arm and raised us both over the bin.

'Any chance you'd like to hear my latest song?' Horace pleaded. 'It's called *Chomper is a Really Top Croc Who Bakes Delicious Pies and has Very Nice Eyes.*'

'I think we've heard enough of your lousy songs for one evening,' Chomper said with a toothy grin. 'As they say in show business,

IT'S CURTAINS FOR YOU TWO!'

Out with the Trash

For those of you who don't know what it feels like to be dropped headfirst into an overflowing garbage bin, I am here to tell you that it is **NOT** a pleasant experience.

Not only is it a messy way to spend a Friday evening, but it is also slimy, sticky, squishy, soggy, saucy, squelchy, stinky and squidgy. Also, it's totally unhygienic.

It didn't help that the bin in question hadn't been emptied for several weeks and a layer of green mould now covered the half-

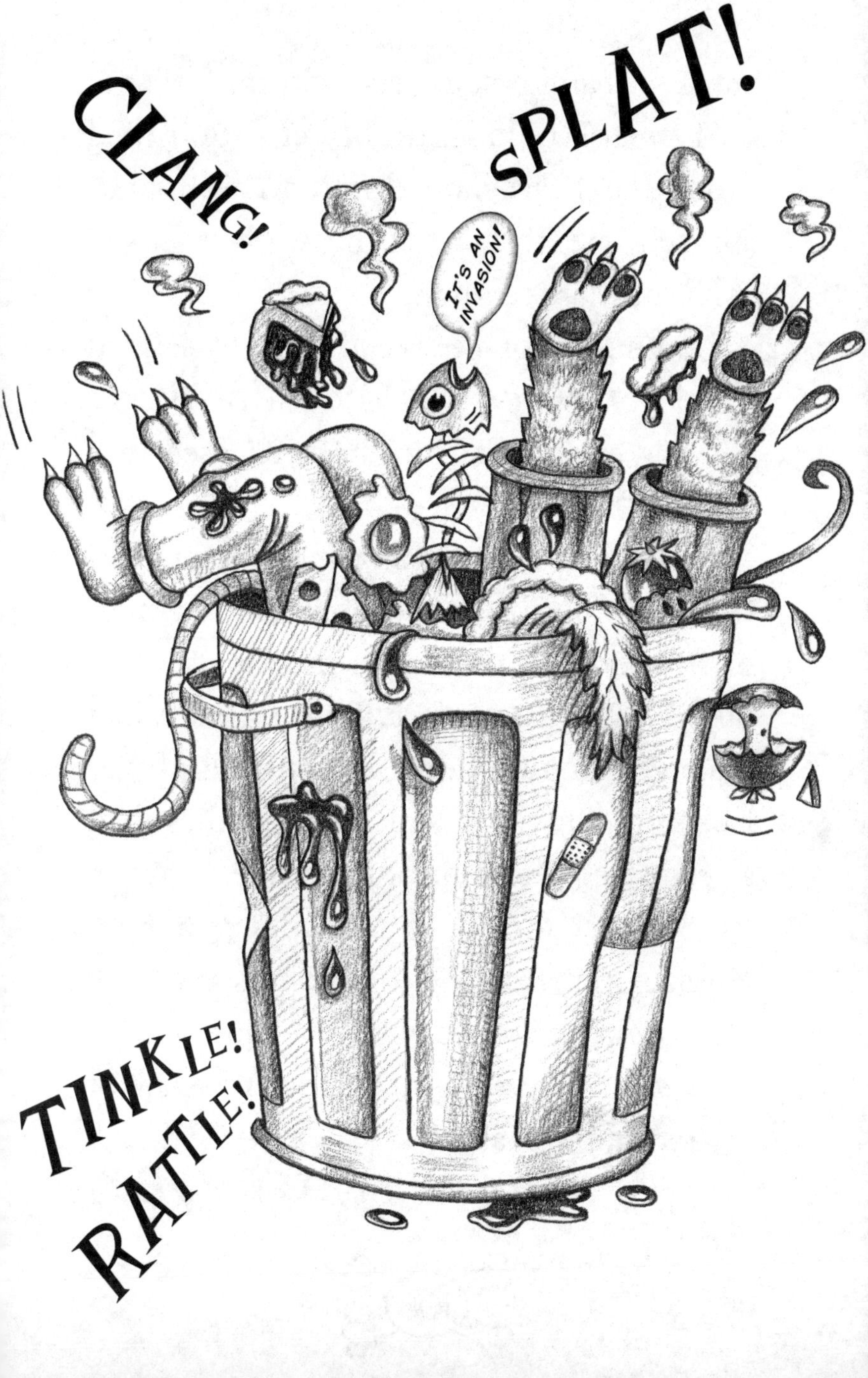

CLANG!
SPLAT!
IT'S AN INVASION!
TINKLE!
RATTLE!

eaten pies and potato peels within.

I swear I could see the bacteria squirming around as I faceplanted into a cheese-and-spinach pie that must have been baked sometime last century.

I'm sure Horace would have exclaimed 'Rotten pies to rotten pies,' had his entire head not been encased in a rotten pie.

With our feet sticking into the air and the rest of our bodies covered in all manner of filth, it took us several minutes to drag ourselves to the surface. By the time I had managed to gulp down a mouthful of pie-free air, Chomper and his buddies had already fled the scene of the crime.

'So much for five-star dining,' ★★★★★ Horace muttered, spitting out something that might once have been a mushroom.

I was more concerned about the state of my recent purchases.

'Let's hope I haven't broken

anything,' I said.

I fished out my not-so-pink carry bag from the bin. Horace's tambourine and triangle attachments were still intact, but Samuel's interpretive dance costume was now a raspberry shade of pink with cherry-red blotches.

I held up the costume.

'Ooogh,' Horace winced. 'That thing is uglier than a sunburnt pig with measles.' He saw the horrified look on my face and added, 'Although, I'm sure Samuel will *lurrrve* it.'

Putting Samuel's costume aside, I reached for my fiddle case. Apart from a layer of squishy pie filling, it appeared to be in one piece.

I placed it in the gutter and carefully opened the lid.

'Wow, that's one ENCHANTED-LOOKING fiddle,' Horace exclaimed.

'Really?' I asked.

'Nah,' Horace said, pointing his hook at the case. 'I just read it on the label. See.'

ENCHANTED
FIDDLE COMPANY

'Oh,' I said, a little disappointed. 'So, it's not really enchanted after all.'

'That all depends how well you can play it,' Horace said. 'Go on, give us a demo.'

'What? You mean now?' I said.

'Why not?' Horace sighed. He gestured to his soiled outfit. 'It's not like they'd let us back in the Pie Palace looking like **THIS**.'

'True,' I said, picking up the fiddle. 'What should I play?'

Horace shot a quick glance at the doorway. 'I'd avoid **Never Smile at a Crocodile**. How about the old Pie Rat ballad **I'm Down in the Dumps 'Cause My Pies are All Gone?**'

'It does suit the mood,' I admitted. I placed the fiddle under my chin and raised the bow. 'Well, here goes.'

I didn't even get through the first verse before Horace was covering his ears and pleading for me to stop. **'ENOUGH! ENOUGH!** You sound like a dying cat in a rubber band factory!'

Not wanting to torture my friend any further, I hurriedly lowered the instrument.

RATTLE!   RATTLE!

'I think your fiddle needs a tiny bit of tuning,' Horace said, uncovering his ears. 'Or maybe a totally new fiddler.'

I was just about to tighten the strings when I heard a *rattling* sound coming from the end of the alley.

I turned to see a small purple octopus dragging an overloaded cart towards us.

I'LL TAKE A SHORTCUT DOWN THIS DARK AND SECLUDED ALLEY ...

A mountain of different-shaped boxes was piled up on the cart labelled:

UNI⋘ CORN SHOP

It seemed that everyone was shopping at Miss Sparkle's store.

I recognised the octopus as a classmate of ours, Owen Undersea. He was a timid little fellow who was constantly being bullied by Chomper O'Many (when Chomper wasn't bullying *me*). Alongside Owen hopped another animal I recognised, Miss Talent Quest herself: Nora Nibblesworth.

'Quick!' Horace hissed. 'Pretend you're a pile of garbage and stand perfectly still.'

I did as Horace instructed and stood motionless in the shadows as Owen and Nora approached.

'Oh, look,' Nora said, catching sight of us. 'It's two homeless buskers pretending to be statues in a *dark* and *secluded alley.*

Give them some money, Owen, before they try to rob us or start playing one of their terrible tunes.'

'**ME?**' Owen said in his squeaky octopus voice. 'But you're the one with all the money.'

Nora rolled her eyes. 'We've already been through this, Owen. I only give money to the poor and needy when there are newspaper reporters watching. Otherwise, what's the point?'

'Oh, all right,' Owen harrumphed. He reached a tentacle into his pocket and removed a tarnished copper coin. 'Here you go, fellas.'

Reluctantly, he tossed the coin into the battered fiddle case as Nora began hopping away.

I continued to stand perfectly still, hoping that Nora hadn't recognised me under six layers of pastry and pie filling.

Horace couldn't resist saying something as Owen took up the strain on his cart.

'Thanks, Owen,' he whispered. 'We'll pay you back on Monday.'

Nora Nibblesworth, who had:

exceptional hearing, along with **exceptional teeth, exceptional whiskers** and

TOP CARROT CRUNCHERS!

exceptionally long eyelashes, spun back to face us and hissed, 'Hook Hand *Hopeless!* Why am I not surprised to find you covered in pie slops? And is that Mischief *McMess,* pretending to be a poor, homeless busker?'

'N-not exactly, Nora,' I said as the **exceptionally** talented bunny hopped closer. 'I mean, it is me, but I wasn't **PRETENDING** to be anything. I was just **PRACTICING** for the talent quest, that's all.'

Nora snatched up Owen's coin.

'In that case, you won't be needing this,' she said, thrusting it into her handbag.

'Hey!' Owen grizzled. 'That was *my* money!'

'Call it a deposit

I'M ON TO YOU!

117

for your assistant's outfit,' Nora said impatiently. 'Fashion doesn't come cheap at the Uni-Corn Shop.'

'Yes, Nora, whatever you say, Nora,' Owen moped.

'That's **Nora the Magnificent** to you,' she snapped. 'Gracious, Owen, how many times do I have to tell you to use my stage name?'

'Sorry, **Nora the Magnificent**,' Owen muttered.

'And while we're on the subject,' Nora went on, 'You'll need to work on your stage presence before tomorrow night. Lots of smiling and waving to the audience, that sort of thing. I can find another assistant if you're not up to the task. There must be **HUNDREDS** of animals on this island – **THOUSANDS** even – who would give up an entire chest of coins to star beside the **magnificently magnificent Nora the Magnificent!'**

Horace leaned in and whispered to me, 'I think this whole **magnificent** thing has gone to Nora's head.'

'You mean it's gone to her **magnificent** head,' I muttered.

Nora rounded on us with an angry look in her eyes. 'What are you two pie-faced buffoons whispering about?'

'Nothing,' Horace said, struggling to hold in a laugh. 'We were just discussing our **magnificent** victory song for the talent quest.'

'Don't waste your time,' Nora sneered. 'Everyone knows whose name will be on that trophy. And it won't be Hook Hand *Horrendous* and Mischief *McFailure*.'

Horace gave me a cheeky wink. 'It's a good thing those **aren't** our names.'

Nora stamped her foot. 'Cut out the comedy, pipsqueak. The fact is that I'm going to **WIN** the Shark Tooth Talent Quest and you're going to come dead *LAST*.'

'Is that so?' Horace said. 'Well, sorry to burst your bubble, Nora, but we've still got a few tricks up our sleeves.'

Using his hook, he pulled a piece of mouldy pie crust from his left sleeve and held it up in triumph.

TA DA!

Nora screwed up her nose. 'That's your **WINNING** routine?'

Horace shrugged and began nibbling on

the pie crust.

I recalled something my Uncle Mutthew had told me after failing his fourth straight audition for Doggy's Got Talent.

'Talent quests **aren't** just about winning,' I said.

'You're right,' Nora agreed. 'They're about winning *convincingly*. No one wants to be the pathetic girl-next-door who won by a whisker. They want to be the champion who *blitzed* her opponents.'

'And isn't that a great message for the girls-next-door of the world,' Horace said through a mouthful of pie crumbs.

DON'T BOTHER TRYING, BECAUSE YOU'LL ALWAYS BE A LOSER.

'I couldn't have said it better myself, Horace,' Nora said.

Horace threw his hook in the air, spitting

out pie crumbs as he spoke.

'I was being **SARCASTIC!'**

Nora ignored him and continued, 'This talent quest is my best opportunity to show the world what a true **CHAMPION** I am. As someone wise once said:

'Winners come and go, but champions last forever.'

'And who said that, exactly?' I asked.

Nora stuck her nose in the air. 'Why, I said it, of course.' And with that, she turned her back on us and began hopping away. 'Come on, Owen, a champion's work is never done.'

With a sigh, Owen wrapped four tentacles around the handle of the cart and trudged after her.

'See ya, guys,' he muttered. 'Good luck with the busking.'

Up and Down

We arrived back at the flying fox, feeling cold, sticky and totally talentless.

The sun had set, and the sky was filled with twinkling stars. In front of us, a tall lamp post lit up the **ARRIVALS LOUNGE**.

'Which one of us should go first?' I said, pointing to the empty seat of the flying fox.

Horace pushed his way through the straw. 'Forget taking turns. I vote we ride **together.'**

'But what about Samuel?' I began.

'Bah! Rotten pies to Samuel,' Horace said with a dismissive wave of his hook. 'By the time that slow-as-a-snail sloth realises we've broken his precious rules, we'll be standing on the tower.'

I spotted a mouse's tail swishing through a nearby patch of straw and wondered what other creepy critters were lurking in there.

'All right,' I agreed. 'It's probably not safe to be waiting down here alone.'

SWISH...

'Smart lad,' Horace said, squeezing beside me on the seat. 'And this way, we'll both have someone to talk to. The ride back to school can be **SOOOO** slow and boring – especially when Samuel is manning the winch.'

He reached up and tugged a short rope. Several seconds later, the flying fox began to move.

'You know what, Horace,' I said, as we reached the roof of the town hall. 'I'd like to win the talent quest, just to teach Nora a lesson.'

'Wouldn't that be something,' Horace whistled. 'I bet Nora has never come **SECOND** in her life.'

'Yeah, and it would be great to *beat* Chomper for a change, instead of Chomper always *beating us up*,' I added.

'Do you think we stand a chance?' Horace asked.

'Benny and Flick have plenty of talent,'

I admitted, 'but I'd need to improve my fiddling if we are to be any match for Chomper, Nora *or* the Salty Seagulls Community Choir. Those guys are born entertainers.'

'Yeah, and my tambourine playing could do with some work,' Horace added. 'It's not easy keeping a beat while trying to look like a ROCK ST★R.' He tilted his head to one side and pulled a ridiculous face. Like most of Horace's expressions, it made him look constipated.

'Err … yes, well, there's no time like the present to start practising,' I said, removing my fiddle from its case. 'It's going to be a **LONG** journey back to school.'

To anyone in the buildings below, it must have sounded like a band of travelling minstrels were holding a concert in the sky. I confess, it wasn't an exceptionally good concert, but our playing did improve the higher we went.

Our tunes became more dramatic as we reached the outskirts of town and began passing through the icy patches of mist blanketing the Bog.

It was a dark and deserted place, and not a sound could be heard from below. Although I doubt I would have heard a STAMPEDE of elephants over the sound of Horace's tambourine playing.

'DO YOU THINK THE HUNGRY HAIRY SEA MONSTER IS DOWN THERE?' I shouted.

Horace gave his tambourine one final shake and then replied, 'I don't believe in the Hungry Hairy Sea Monster.'

'Well, if you did believe in it, do you think it would be roaming the Bog tonight?' I asked.

'Hmm,' Horace considered. 'The moon is

full, the tide is out and there is plenty of mist, so **YES**, if I were a mythical sea monster, I'd be on the prowl for a tasty morsel to eat.'

'You don't suppose the Hungry Hairy Sea Monster likes the taste of *dog*, do you?' I asked apprehensively.

Horace shook his head. 'No one likes the taste of dog, Mischief. Unless you're referring to dog-and-gravy pie. I've heard those things are to die for!'

I felt my ears *drooping*.

'Don't worry,' Horace said, seeing the horrified look on my face. 'You're too gristly for pie filling. Although when it comes to hot dogs and sausages, they do say that anything goes.'

I'M ONE *HOT* DOG!

'That's hardly a comforting thought,' I said. 'Next you'll be telling me they put dog's tails in sausage rolls.'

'Now, now, don't get your knickerbockers in a knot,' Horace said. 'If it makes you so upset, I'll promise not to talk about:

HOT DOGS,
DOG PIES,
BARBECUE DOG,
DOG STEW,
DOG SORBET,
FRIED DOG'S PAWS,
DOG EAR SURPRISE
or any other
DOG-RELATED CUISINE.'

DOG STEW –
EEEYEWWW!

There was a brief silence.

'But I'm still allowed to talk about **DOGFISH PIE,'** Horace blurted out. 'It's not technically dog and it goes well with a nice tartare sauce. That reminds me, I was supposed to bring back a fishatarian pie for Flick. No sauce –'

130

'Shh,' I hissed.

'Oh, don't be like that, Mischief,' Horace said. 'Surely you don't have a problem with fishatarian pies.'

'No,' I whispered. 'I think I can *hear* something.'

'Like what?' Horace said. 'I can't *hear* anything.'

'That's because you haven't stopped *talking!*'

'Oh, right,' Horace said, shutting his mouth.

From somewhere far below came a faint *whistle*. It sounded like wind blowing through long hair, or a gentle sea breeze rustling the needles of a clifftop pine tree. I knew for certain there were *no* pine trees growing in the Bog.

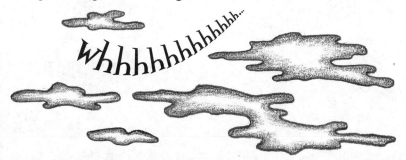

'SHIVER ME SEA MONSTERS!'

Horace exclaimed, jerking his body in the direction of the sound. 'There **IS** a Hungry Hairy Sea Monster!'

Horace was rather uncoordinated when it came to his new hook hand and he forgot that he had a large tambourine stuck to the end of his arm. As he spun in panic, the tambourine **STRUCK** the neck of my fiddle.

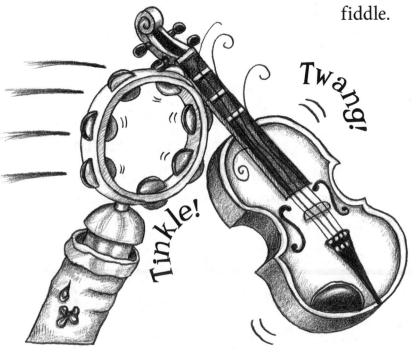

With the twang of strings and the tinkle of bells, the fiddle was torn from my grasp.

Before I had time to regain my grip, the fiddle had disappeared into the mist below.

I was left clutching a bow in one paw and empty dreams in the other.

'Whoops,' Horace muttered as the eerie whistling sound continued to echo though the mist.

Whhhhhhhhhhh...

Looking rather guilty, he held out his new triangle attachment. 'You could always try a different instrument. I've heard the triangle is easy to master.' He gave it a little *TING!*

I peered down into the grey nothingness, unsure whether to cry or to send a certain unwanted passenger plunging down after the fiddle. My musical

career was over before it had begun.

Just like my Uncle Mutthew, I thought. *I'm just another failure in a family of failures.*

Horace gestured to several glowing shapes in the mist in front of us.

'At least we made it safely back to school,' he said cheerfully.

I struggled to see the positive side to what had been a complete and utter disaster. I had **spent** all my birthday money, *lost* my fiddle, was *covered* in rotten pie and I *hadn't* even had a bite to eat. Worse still, the strange whistling sound continued to play like a mournful funeral tune.

How fitting, I thought. *My hopes of winning the talent quest are well and truly dead.*

Excuses

As the flaming torches of the tower came into view, the ghostly whistling sound was replaced by the **panting** and *puffing* of Samuel winding the winch.

PHEW!

Drawing closer, I spotted Flick and Benny waiting on the tower with Sir Squawk-a-lot. Flick was adding the finishing touches to a cardboard sun around the toucan's neck. She had clearly started the costume fitting without us.

The lemon-yellow sun did little to **brighten** my mood.

'What in the name of Blacktail the Bold hast happened to thee?' Sir Squawk-a-lot chirped in his ridiculous medieval voice.

'Chomper happened, that's what happened,' Horace said. He tumbled out of the seat, scattering pie crumbs and rotten pie filling all over the cobblestones.

I hurriedly handed Samuel his dance costume before the sloth had a chance to lecture me about riding DOUBLE.

I made a solemn vow to always ride **SOLO** in the future.

'I hope you like the costume, Samuel,' I said, trying to sound excited.

'Ahhh … **PINK** …' Samuel said, holding the tutu up to his waist. 'My … *favourite* … colour …' Lost in thought, he slowly shuffled down the stairs.

'We won't charge you extra for the berry stains,' Horace called after him. 'Now, if the rest of you will excuse me, I'm off to have a bubble bath, and a slice of pie for supper.'

'Speaking of pies,' Flick began, 'didn't I put in an order for –'

'A fishatarian pie, yes, I know,' Horace said. 'And I had the perfect pie picked out for you. Truly I did. Extra sardines. No sauce. You would have **LOVED** it.'

'So where is it now?' Flick pressed.

'Err, that's a long story,' Horace said. 'But it ends with Chomper and a dark alleyway.'

'If it's any consolation, I didn't get any pie, either,' I added.

'And what about your *fiddle?*' Flick said, gesturing to my empty case. 'Is Chomper responsible for its disappearance, too?'

'Not exactly,' I said, with a quick glance at Horace. 'It kind of slipped through my fingers.'

Flick stuck her paint-splattered paws on her hips.

'Really, Mischief!' she said crossly. 'You should learn to be more responsible. We're all relying on your fiddling skills to **WIN** the talent quest.'

'H-here's the thing,' I stammered. 'The fiddle, it well … you see …'

'IT FELL INTO THE BOG,' Horace burst out. 'Yes, I confess, it was all my fault. I'm the clumsy klutz. I'm

the rodent in rehab. I'm the rat with the troublesome tambourine.'

'So, are you volunteering to retrieve it?' Flick asked.

'Rotten pies, no!' Horace exclaimed. 'There's no way on earth I'm going down to the Bog in the middle of the night with that strange whistling creature on the prowl.'

'I thought you didn't believe in the Hungry Hairy Sea Monster,' Benny said.

'I didn't,' Horace replied. 'I mean, I don't. I mean, there is **SOMETHING** down there. And in my experience, any creature that chooses to live in a sewage-smelling swamp has got to be nasty.'

'Don't rats live in sewage-smelling swamps?' Benny asked.

'Feral rats, yes,' Horace replied. 'But I'm a sophistimocated Pie Rat. We prefer to hang around trendy pie shops and bright, cheerful places, not dark, monster-ridden bogs.'

SOPHISTIMOCATED PIE RAT

LIKES:
· TRENDY PIE SHOPS
· EATING WITH CUTLERY
· TALKING ABOUT SOPHISTIMOCATED THINGS

DISLIKES:
· FERAL PIE RATS
· CATS WITH POOR CONVERSATIONAL SKILLS
· SEWERS

pwwarrp...

FERAL PIE RAT

LIKES:
· MOULDY PIES
· EATING WITH FINGERS
· SEWAGE-SMELLING SWAMPS

DISLIKES:
· SOPHISTIMOCATED PIE RATS
· WEARING PANTS
· BUBBLE BATHS
· TABLE MANNERS

'Oh, don't be so dramatic,' Flick said. 'Just because the sun has gone down, doesn't mean there's a bogeyman on the loose.'

'This has nothing to do with the darkness,' Horace argued. 'In fact, I flatly refuse to go anywhere near the Bog during the **DAY** or the **NIGHT.**'

'Well, someone will have to fetch that fiddle,' Flick persisted. 'We've designed the entire act around it.'

'Mischief even has his own fiddling solo,' Benny added. 'Right after the line, **Hey diddle diddle, the dog rocks the fiddle.**'

'And thou must not forget his specially designed moon costume,' Sir Squawk-a-lot said, sweeping his wing through the air. 'It helps him fly across the stage as he plays.'

'Sorry to let you down,' I said. 'But I don't like our chances of finding a TINY fiddle in a dark, gloomy bog.'

'Why don't we send Flick?' Horace said. 'She has excellent night vision.'

Flick narrowed her green eyes at him.

'On second thoughts,' Horace said, 'perhaps she's a scaredy cat like the rest of us.'

Flick let out a loud **HISS!**

'Black cats aren't afraid of the dark. We just hate to get our paws **WET!'**

IT'S A
PUDDLE!
EEEEK!

SPLASH!

Horace turned to the chimp. 'And what about you, Benny?'

'Me?' Benny spluttered. 'Um, well … chimps are allergic to bog water.'

'Since when?' Horace pressed.

'Since, err … last Sunday,' Benny began.

'It's all right,' I broke in. 'I'll go. It's **my** fiddle, so it's **my** responsibility.'

Horace patted me on the shoulder. 'How very noble of you, Mischief. Now, if you'll excuse me, I hear a bubble bath calling my name, *gurgle, gurgle, Horace...*'

He spun on his heel and began scampering towards the stairwell.

'Hang on, Horace,' Flick called after him, a guilty tone to her voice. 'Perhaps we should visit the Bog together.'

'*Together?*' Horace exclaimed, skidding to a halt. 'Are you seriously suggesting we *ALL* get eaten by the Hungry Hairy Sea Monster?'

'No,' Flick said. 'I'm saying that this is a **team** performance, and we should do things as a **team.** You know, strength in numbers and all that safety hoo-ha. Mischief would do the same for us.'

'The fair damsel doth have a point,' Sir Squawk-a-lot chirped.

'Oh, all right,' Horace said, trudging back across the tower. 'All for **one** and **one** for getting out of that Bog as quickly as possible!'

'Thanks, Horace,' I murmured.

'But I insist we bring a cannon,' Horace said. 'A really **BIG** cannon.'

'And plenty of bananas,' Benny added. 'They're the perfect survival food for dangerous missions.'

Flick turned to face the toucan. 'Perhaps you should stay here and keep a lookout. We'll signal with a lantern if we're in any trouble. Tell the headmaster to send a search party if we haven't returned by dawn.'

'Thy wish is my command, fair maiden,' Sir Squawk-a-lot said. He attempted to bow in his cardboard sun, but smeared wet, yellow paint all over his feathers.

'And if you hear me SCREAMING like a baby, you are to fly down at once and pluck me from the jaws of death,' Horace insisted.

'My ears will be on high alert,' the toucan promised.

'Good,' Horace said. 'Now, if we hurry, we might get back before the other students use all the hot water and I'm forced to take an *ICE* bath.'

'You'll be wanting more than a bath after a visit to the Bog,' Benny said, making his way down the tower. 'The mud in that place is stickier than mashed banana. And don't get me started on the smell ...'

A Smelly, Muddy Visit to the Bog

The Bog was, in a word, *boggy*.

I couldn't *see* much through the dense layer of mist, but I sure could *feel* what lay under my feet. *Mashed banana* was an accurate description.

Flick had insisted that she wear her knee-high boots to keep her precious toes dry.

BIG mistake.

Her boots disappeared into the mud in less time than it took Horace to say, 'Hey, is

that a brown sea cucumber, or the remains of yesterday's lunch?'

I confess, it was hard to tell the difference between the wildlife of the Bog and what came out of the SOS sewage pipe.

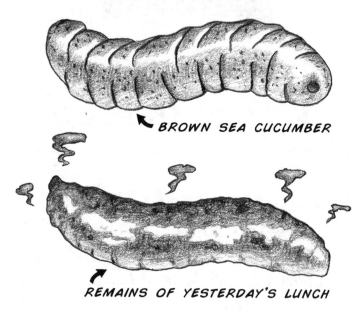

BROWN SEA CUCUMBER

REMAINS OF YESTERDAY'S LUNCH

'The Hungry Hairy Sea Monster is not the only thing we have to worry about,' Benny warned as we squelched through the putrid muck. 'I've heard this place is filled with sinkholes, sea snakes and killer quicksand!'

'Not to mention **killer seaweed!**' Horace added, poking a cautious toe into a nearby puddle.

'Since when was seaweed on the killer vegetable list?' Flick asked suspiciously.

Horace pointed to his stumpy legs. 'Everything is a potential killer when you're as short as me! If I get tangled up in a patch of seaweed I could be dragged under the surface, contract a deadly seaweed virus … or worse.'

'I'm sure Benny can piggyback you if we run into any **killer seaweed**,' Flick said. 'Now, let's get a move on before the tide washes Mischief's fiddle out to sea and we have to contend with **KILLER WHALES.**'

We ventured further into the Bog, following the line of the flying fox. Flick carried our only lantern, which remained

unlit. There was plenty of moonlight to see where we were going, and it was safer **NOT** to give our location away with a potential sea monster on the prowl.

We reached the spot where I thought I had dropped the fiddle and began searching the shallow water.

It should have been easy, considering that my fiddle was made of **wood,** and wood **floats.** But we were soon splattered with mud and other unmentionable substances, with nothing to show for our troubles.

Our only comfort was that we hadn't heard the strange whistling sound since leaving the school.

'Are you certain you dropped your fiddle **HERE?**' Flick asked impatiently.

'I'm not a hundred percent confident,' I confessed.

'Maybe we should try another spot,' Benny said. 'Which way should we go, Mischief? You're the dog with the detective's nose.'

I raised my head and took an enormous sniff of the foul-scented air. My nose immediately began to tingle. It was a sensation I got whenever I sensed **DANGER,** whenever something was **WRONG,** or whenever there was a **TRAIL** to follow. The problem was I could never tell *what* had triggered the tingle.

I crossed my fingers and hoped I was on the trail of the fiddle and not an overly stinky sea cucumber.

'This way,' I said, stepping into the mist.

We walked in silence for some time, Benny leading the way. He was humming a new rap to himself, and I managed to catch a few verses. It wasn't his greatest gangster rap by any stretch of the imagination.

Mud, mud, mud.
Mud, mud, mud.
Mud, mud, mud.
Everywhere mud.

The **SECOND** verse was the same as the **FIRST** verse, which was the same as the **THIRD** verse. The **FOURTH** verse sounded suspiciously similar.

When Benny reached the **FIFTH** verse, he added a new line.

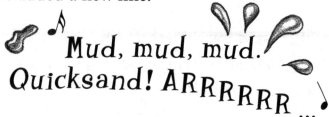

Mud, mud, mud.
Quicksand! ARRRRRR ...

Judging by the panic in Benny's voice, I feared the worst and quickened my pace to catch up with him.

My fears were confirmed when I found Benny standing knee-deep in a patch of **killer quicksand.** He was sinking quickly.

'Help,' he groaned. 'Get me out of here.'

Dropping to my knees, I scrambled to the edge of the quicksand and stretched out my arm. My fingers brushed the tips of Benny's ringed fingers, but I couldn't quite reach him.

'**QUICK, MISCHIEF!**' he hollered as his body continued to sink. 'Find a piece of driftwood.'

I glanced around me. There wasn't a piece of driftwood in sight. In fact, all I could see was a small bush and a brown sea cucumber. At least I *THOUGHT* it was a brown sea cucumber.

I AM NOT A BROWN SEA CUCUMBER!

Ignoring the brown, sticky object, I scrambled to my feet and rushed over to the bush. I attempted to rip the entire thing out of the ground, but its roots extended deep into the mud and it refused to budge.

If only I were a little stronger, I thought in frustration. For the second time that day, I wished the SOS gym hadn't been turned into a torture chamber.

Flick and Horace arrived to see Benny waist-deep in the quicksand and floundering around like a moth in candle wax.

'I see you've found the killer quicksand,'
Horace said calmly.

'Don't just stand there, Captain Obvious!'
Benny shouted. 'Pass me your **SCISSOR
SWORD!**'

'Sorry, Benny,' Horace said, touching his empty belt. 'But, you know the SOS rule about carrying dangerous weapons at school.'

'But this isn't **SCHOOL!**' Benny screamed. 'It's a patch of **killer quicksand!**'

'Well, I still can't offer you my sword,' Horace said. 'I left it under my bed. How about a lantern?'

Before Flick could stop him, Horace had snatched the lantern out of her grasp.

Despite his noble intentions, Horace chose to use his wayward hook hand for the manoeuvre. The lantern slid **STRAIGHT** off the end of his hook, **spun** in a circle and splashed into the quicksand with a **PLOP!** There was a *gurgle, gurgle, swishhhh* as it sank beneath the surface.

swishhhhhhh...

'Whoops,' Horace said as the shiny object disappeared from sight. 'I guess we won't be signalling Sir Squawk-a-lot in a hurry.'

Flick looked ready to throw Horace into the quicksand.

Benny continued to sink.

'**HURRY!**' he cried, as the quicksand reached his shoulders. 'I'm almost under!'

'Just hold on!' I said, trying to remain calm, but failing miserably. 'I think we passed an old plank back there. Maybe we can –'

The words caught in my throat.

My legs froze in terror.

My nose began to *tingle* as I stared

into the moonlit night.

Rising out of the mist behind Benny was an enormous shaggy shape.

Blacktail have mercy, I gasped. *It's the Hungry Hairy Sea Monster.*

The Hungry Hairy Sea Monster

Horace let out a startled **SQUEAK** and darted behind the bush.

'Don't move a muscle, Benny,' I whispered.

'Don't move? What kind of useless advice is that?' Benny said. 'I'm up to my **neck** in quicksand. I couldn't move a muscle even if I wanted to.'

'Quicksand isn't all you have to worry about,' Flick said, her eyes locked on the

mist.

'Then what –?' Benny began. He took one look at the terrified expression on Flick's face and turned whiter than a snowman. **The H-H-Hungry H-H-Hairy S-S-Sea Monster is creeping up behind me, isn't it?'**

'There is something creeping up behind you,' Flick said. 'And it does look suspiciously **HAIRY.'**

'Though it might not be **HUNGRY**,' I reassured him.

'Oooh! It's hungry all right,' Horace squealed. 'I can feel it in my bones!'

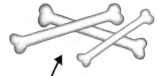

HORACE'S BONES (SMALL AND UNRELIABLE)

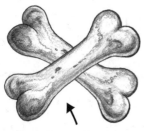

MISCHIEF'S BONES (SOMETIMES RELIABLE)

'Your bones are SMALL and unreliable,' Flick hissed. 'Leave this to the experts!'

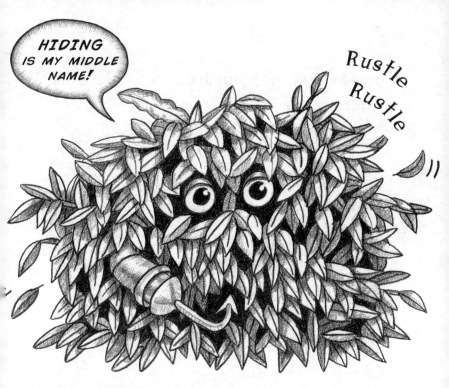

'With pleasure,' Horace said, burrowing further into the bush.

A small part of me felt like joining him. A bigger part of me felt like running in the opposite direction yelling, **'HELP! HELP!** There's a dog-eating monster on the loose!'

But as one of the so-called *experts*, I held my ground, hoping that the creature had filled its belly with SOS toilet waste and was

now looking for a suitable spot to take a nap
– or to vomit.

'Is it still there?' Benny whispered.

I blinked several times, hoping the
shadowy shape was just a trick of the light.

The creature refused to disappear.

'It's still there,' I said, then added
wishfully, 'though perhaps it has poor vision
and will mistake your head for a coconut.'

'I bet it's got **HUGE,
gOOgly** sea-
monster eyes with
MONSTERRIFIC
night vision,'
Horace blurted
out.

'And how would you know a thing like that?' Flick hissed. 'You can't see a thing from inside that bush.'

'Call it my **SIXTH SENSE**,' Horace said.

'More like your **NONSENSE**,' Flick muttered.

'Err, guys,' Benny quavered. 'I can feel the monster's breath on the back of my neck!'

He was right. The Hungry Hairy Sea Monster was right behind him. It lumbered along on four legs – a dark, shaggy silhouette, shaking the ground with every step.

THUMP!

THUMP!

THUMP!

If Shark Tooth Island had a prize for the stinkiest creature, the Hungry Hairy Sea Monster would win, paws down.

I covered my nose to block out the foul aroma of decaying seaweed, raw sewage and wet fur.

'They should change that thing's name to the Really Stinky Sea Monster!' Horace gagged from the bush.

'Any last-minute song requests?' Benny said, as the monster reached the edge of the quicksand. 'Or should I start composing my own funeral rap?'

'Sing a song about roses,' Horace spluttered.

'Anything to take my mind off that smell!' The monster lowered its head. In the pale moonlight, I glimpsed a large wet nose and two enormous horns. The creature's eyes were concealed behind a mop of shaggy, brown hair, but there was no mistaking the LONG strands of seaweed draped over its back.

Its mouth began to open.

I was powerless to stop it.

'*Oooooooooo!*' Benny wailed. 'It's gonna peel me like a banana, or bite off one of my ears!'

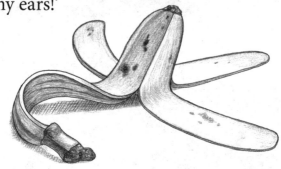

But the monster did not peel Benny like a banana. Nor did it nibble on one of his ears. It simply clamped its massive jaws around the back of Benny's school tracksuit and began hauling him out of the quicksand.

'Errrr, w-w-what's happening?' Benny spluttered in confusion.

'I think it's trying to **rescue** you,' I said in wonder.

'Either that or it intends to carry you off to its den, where you will be slowly roasted

over white-hot coals and *then* peeled like a banana!' Horace piped.

Flick glared down at the bush. 'Do you ever have anything **HELPFUL** to say, Horace?'

Horace muttered something **UNHELPFUL** and went back into hiding.

When Benny's legs and toes had finally cleared the surface of the quicksand, the monster opened its jaws and dropped the soggy chimp onto the ground.

Picking himself up, Benny hurriedly scrambled over to us, trailing wet sand behind him.

'BRUISED BANANAS!' he panted. 'I thought I was done for!'

I stared at the strange creature.

'I guess the Hungry Hairy Sea Monster doesn't like the taste of quicksand-covered chimps,' I said.

The shaggy beast stared back at me. At least I *think* it was staring back at me. I couldn't see its eyes under all that hair.

It remained hushed for a moment, then raised its nose high into the air and let out a mighty:

Flick shot me a sideways glance.

'That was unexpected,' she exclaimed.

'I guess *moo* is sea monster speak for *hello*,' I said, perplexed.

'But sea monsters don't say *moo*,' Horace squeaked from inside the bush.

THEY GO ROAR, OR SCREECH, OR GURGLE, GURGLE, CHOMP!

'Well this one goes *moo*,' I said, peering closer at the strange animal.

Flick's eyes lit up with realisation.

'That's because it's not a sea monster!' she exclaimed. 'Look! Under all that seaweed. I think it's a

...COW!'

Hairy Highland Cows

Flick was right. If you were to take away the seaweed and give the creature a good bath, you would be left with something that roughly resembled a cow.

Horace had his doubts.

'A cow?' he exclaimed, poking his nose out from between the branches. 'But that thing is too *hairy* to be a cow.'

'I think it's one of those hairy highland cows Mrs Nibblesworth told us about in zoology class,' Flick said. 'The Scottish call them *coos*.'

'Err, I might have nodded off during that lesson,' Horace confessed. 'But I'll take your word for it.'

FACT HAIRY COOS COME FROM THE HIGHLANDS OF SCOTLAND.

MRS NIBBLESWORTH
(FULL OF FACTS)

'So, what is this one doing in the LOWLANDS of the Bog?' Benny asked.

'BAGPIPES!'
BOOMED A LOUD VOICE.

'Shiver me tartan kilts!' Horace exclaimed, shaking the bush in panic. 'It can talk!'

'Of course, I can talk, my wee laddie,' the monster said in a thick Scottish accent. 'I just prefer silence.'

He blew a clump of hair out of his eyes and began munching on the closest leaves of the bush.

Horace frantically untangled himself and scrambled to safety before he lost another body part to a hungry animal.

The four of us stood in a line, mouths agape, staring at the hairy cow as he stripped leaves off the bush. He might not have been the Hungry Hairy Sea Monster, but he certainly was **HUNGRY.**

'Psst,' Horace whispered. 'Did he just mention **bagpipes?**'

'I-I think so,' I said, unsure whether to trust my own ears or to dismiss the entire evening as one bizarre dream.

'But there aren't any bagpipes in the Bog,' Horace said. 'Or on Shark Tooth Island.'

'Precisely,' the cow said, looking up from the bush. 'And that is why I immigrated to Shark Tooth Island from the highlands of Scotland. To escape the cursed Scottish bagpipes!'

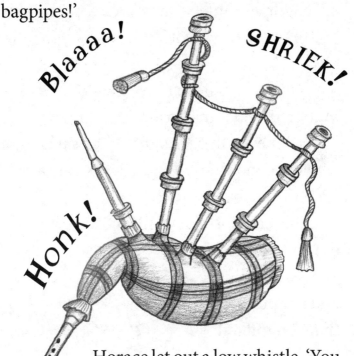

Blaaaa!

SHRIEK!

Honk!

Horace let out a low whistle. 'You must really hate bagpipes to live in this dump of a place!'

'Aye,' the cow said. 'Bagpipes drive me CRAZY. All that blaring and screeching and high-pitched shrieking. The noise is deafening. I much prefer the solitude of the Bog. Peace and quiet. Ahh, that's the

bonnie life for me. No visitors and definitely no bagpipers infecting my ears with their poisonous tunes. Nothing but sweet, calm bliss.'

'**STINKY** bliss, more like it,' Horace muttered under his breath.

'Let me get this straight,' Flick said. 'This whole sea monster business is just a sham to keep the noisy bagpipers away.'

'The bagpipers *and* the noisy students,' the cow snorted. 'You Scallywags make more noise than a highland marching band in a thunderstorm – especially during talent quest rehearsals.'

'Speaking of the talent quest,' I said, 'you haven't perchance seen a $fiddle$ lying around, have you?'

The hairy highland cow stepped away from the bush, which was now just a collection of bare twigs.

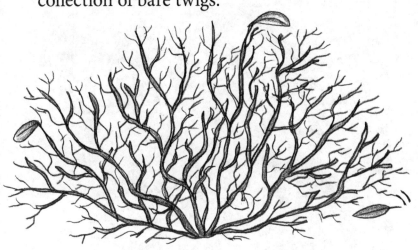

'Aye, laddie,' he said. 'I picked one up on my evening garbage run. You'd be surprised at how many things get dropped from the flying fox. I've collected an entire bookshelf of SOS library books, not to mention three barrels of silver coins and seven matchstick model ships.'

DANGER!
HIGHLY
FLAMMABLE

He began fossicking around in his seaweed disguise. 'Hmm, the fiddle is in here somewhere …'

After pulling out one of Flick's boots, two pie crusts and a couple of zoology text books, he eventually located my fiddle – well, what was left of my fiddle.

What tiny spark of magic my **enchanted** fiddle had once contained was now well and truly gone. The fall from the flying fox had knocked the heart and soul out of it. The neck had been snapped in two and the strings stuck out like catfish whiskers after an electric eel attack.

I felt totally **DISenchanted**.

'It's beyond repair,' I thought with drooping ears. *'And I am a picture of despair.'*

'Hey, that rhymes,' Benny said.

'Oh,' I said, realising that I must have spoken the words aloud. 'Well, too bad. A good rhyme needs a good melody, and I doubt I could compose *any* melody without

my fiddle.'

The hairy cow gave me a sympathetic look. Or perhaps he was considering eating me for dessert. I've never been good at reading cow expressions.

'Perhaps you'd consider a trade,' he said. 'One of my *quieter* instruments for your fiddle. The strings would make a fine hair tie for my wife, Aggie. She's forever complaining about getting long locks of hair in her eyes.'

'Oh, so there are **TWO** Hungry Hairy Sea Monsters roaming the Bog?' Horace said, glancing around nervously. 'What a comforting thought.'

'There are **FOUR** monsters to be precise,' the cow clarified. 'Yours truly, my dear wife, Aggie, and our wee children, Angus and Agnes. They're a right pair of troublemakers, those two. Always getting into dung fights and raiding rubbish bins in the

middle of the
night. Bless their
precious souls.'

'They sound
suspiciously like
TWO Scallywags
I know,' Flick
said, with a
quick frown at
Horace and me.

'Hey! We weren't in
that bin by choice,' Horace protested. 'And
it was twilight, not the middle of the night.'

'Back to this whole instrument thing,' I
said. 'I don't suppose you have anything we
could use for our talent quest performance?'

'That depends on your act,' the cow said.

'It's a **Sea Shanty Gangster
Rap**,' Benny explained.

'Urgh,' the cow coughed. 'I hate those
things. They're always so loud and rude.'

'Yeah, but this one is about *you*,' Horace

pointed out.

'Me?' the cow said in surprise. 'Well, dress me in a kilt and serve me up as haggis! In that case I'm a *fan*. What an honour. I was beginning to fear the entire island had forgotten about the Hungry Hairy Sea Monster. This will certainly keep the legend alive.' He lowered his voice to a whisper.

'Between you and me, the only thing stopping the mayor from turning my beloved Bog into a *three-story concert hall* with *underground boat parking* and *twenty-four-hour bagpiping shows* is the legend of the Hungry Hairy Sea Monster.'

WELCOME TO BOGWORLD
HOME OF BAGPIPES

Blaaaa! Honk! SHRIEK!

'As long as the legend lives on, the Broadway producers refuse to venture anywhere near this place.'

'Oh,' he added, 'if you could avoid using the words COW, COO or CATTLE in your performance I would be eternally grateful. MONSTER has a much scarier ring to it.'

'Monster it is,' Benny promised. 'Your secret will remain our secret.'

'Good,' the cow-turned-monster said. 'Now, back to your instrument. I have something that is guaranteed to send tingles down the spines of every member of your audience.'

'What is it?' Horace asked excitedly.

The cow removed a small water-reed panpipe from around his neck. 'This wee instrument creates the sound of the Hungry Hairy Sea Monster.'

whhhhhhhhhh...

Final Preparations

It was the evening of the talent quest and my stomach was filled with **butterflies**. Some of them had escaped and were flying around the spotlights. Although on closer inspection, I think they were **moths**.

OH LOOK, A PRETTY LIGHT!

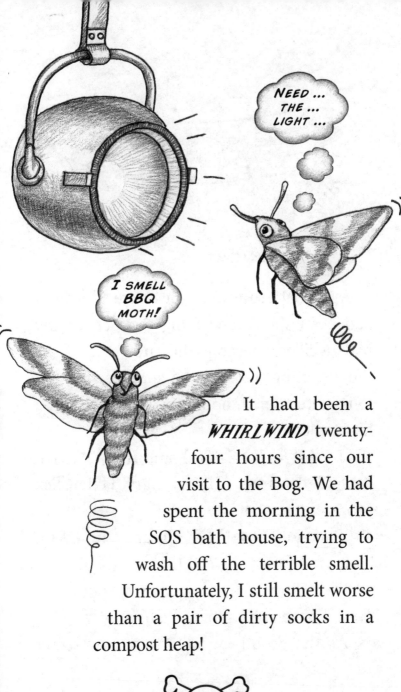

It had been a *WHIRLWIND* twenty-four hours since our visit to the Bog. We had spent the morning in the SOS bath house, trying to wash off the terrible smell. Unfortunately, I still smelt worse than a pair of dirty socks in a compost heap!

drip...

With bath time over, the entire afternoon had been spent rehearsing our act. Benny had decided to scrap the first half of his rap, pointing out that the audience wanted to be entertained, not bored to death with a history lesson.

'DRAMA, MYSTERY and INTRIGUE!' he had declared. 'The Hungry Hairy Sea Monster has it all.'

'Plus, lots of hair,' Horace chimed in. 'You can't forget the hair.'

'Yes, Horace,' Benny groaned, rolling his eyes. 'I haven't forgotten the hair.'

As the proud owner of our new secret

weapon, I had been put in charge of sound effects.

My panpipe was a curious instrument, constructed from water reeds of various lengths and arranged in a line. By blowing air through each reed, different notes were created. Together, the notes formed a tune.

In some ways, my panpipe was similar to a bagpipe, but much QUIETER and far less annoying. While bagpipes made a **DEAFENING** screeching sound, my panpipe made a soft, whistling sound, which was swept across the Bog by the

gentlest of breezes. For years, the sound had been mistaken for wind rustling through the Hungry Hairy Sea Monster's long hair.

It was certainly a clever trick.

I lacked the skill to conjure up a thrilling orchestral piece on my instrument, but I did manage to compose a humble little ditty called THE MARCH OF THE SEA CUCUMBERS.

Horace suggested I call it THE MARCH OF THE SOS SEWAGE PIPE, but Benny pointed out that sewage pipes didn't technically *march*, they slowly oozed. He also informed me that THE SLOW OOZE OF THE SOS SEWAGE PIPE was a little too long-winded (as well as *foul*-winded) for a title.

I would have liked several more days to

perfect my piece, or perhaps an entire month, but the occasional missed note added to the **GHOSTLY** appeal of the song.

With the panpipe safely hidden under my blazer, I waited backstage with my friends as the audience began taking their seats.

The Sea Shanty Theatre had an open-air stage, which overlooked the school oval.

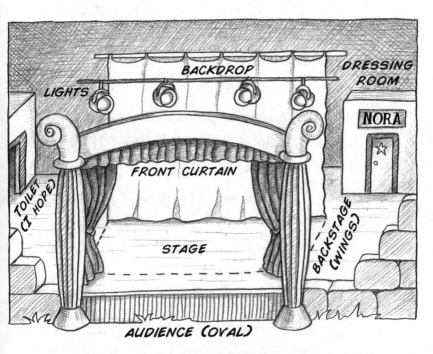

PLAN OF THE SEA SHANTY THEATRE

Old Fetch had set up wooden chairs on the grass and there was a cart selling hot chips beneath the fig tree. The statue of Blacktail the Bold looked on from the lilypond. His elephant trunk had been removed and his tail once again squirted out dirty, black pondwater.

The other acts milled around us, speaking in whispered voices and making last-minute adjustments to their costumes.

Samuel looked radiant in his pretty pink leotard and tutu. Nora the Magnificent looked relaxed in her private dressing room.

Chomper looked positively **TERRIFYING** with his collection of nasty knives. He looked up from his knife sharpening and growled, 'Ready to embarrass yourself, *McFailure?*'

Truth be told, I was ready to make a complete and utter **goose** out of myself, but I decided not to admit it.

'I see they're saving the **BEST** for last,' Horace said, pointing at the run sheet.

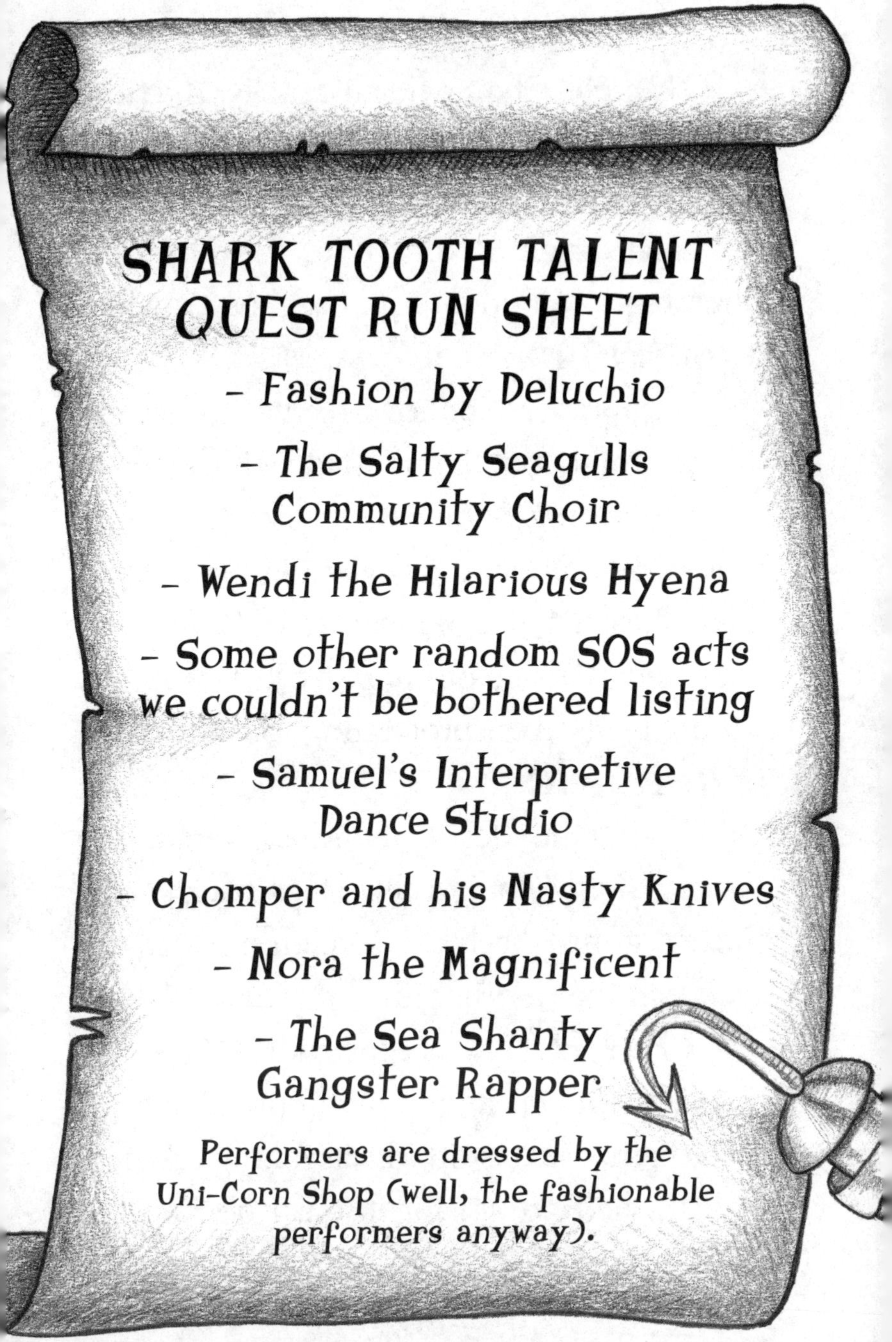

SHARK TOOTH TALENT QUEST RUN SHEET

- Fashion by Deluchio

- The Salty Seagulls Community Choir

- Wendi the Hilarious Hyena

- Some other random SOS acts we couldn't be bothered listing

- Samuel's Interpretive Dance Studio

- Chomper and his Nasty Knives

- Nora the Magnificent

- The Sea Shanty Gangster Rapper

Performers are dressed by the Uni-Corn Shop (well, the fashionable performers anyway).

'Humph,' Chomper snorted. 'By the time you fleabags hit the stage, the competition will be well and truly over.'

'That's right,' Nora cried through her dressing room door. 'And I will be crowned **CHAMPION!**'

Chomper looked ready to argue the point, but he spotted Miss Sparkle approaching Nora with a bucket of carrots and shot me an angry glare instead.

'Just stay out of my way, *McFailure,*' he warned. 'Or one of my nasty knives might find themselves protruding out of your **backside.**'

Having no desire to be skewered like a corn dog, I took a few steps backwards, pricking my heel on something wedged between the floorboards.

'**OUCH,**' I winced, bending down to pick it up. It was a long metal pin; the type wagoners use to stop wheels falling off their axels. I had no use for it, but I pocketed it all the same, if only to save me from pricking my heel a **SECOND** time.

When the audience members were finally seated, the master of ceremonies, Professor Porkchop, clomped onto the stage, to the sound of polite applause.

CLOMP CLOMP CLOMP clap clap clap

The school's chef had swapped his egg-splattered apron for a ridiculous white tuxedo. He still wore his cauliflower chef's hat, which made him look like the host of a celebrity cooking competition. The barrel of Apple Fizz* he used as a peg leg sounded unusually *FULL* for a Saturday evening, though I suspected it would be **EMPTY** by the end of the night.

---

*Note to parents: Apple Fizz does not contain alcohol. It does, however, contain large amounts of sugar and bubbles. Children are discouraged from drinking more than eleven glasses before bedtime.

'Welcome, me hearties, to this year's Shark Tooth Talent Quest,' he announced with a loud snort. 'We are gathered on this auspicious occasion to celebrate the achievements of SOS's most *gifted* students. But before the snot-nosed brats take to the stage, it is my great pleasure to introduce our three judges, **Madam Melody, Legs Lorraine** and our very own **Headmaster von Ironheart!**'

On cue, a spotlight lit up the three judges in the front row. In the harsh light, Legs Lorraine's canary-yellow string bikini looked even **GHASTLIER** than usual.

Horace covered his eyes with his hook and moaned, 'I've been scarred for life …'

Professor Porkchop continued, 'It is the judges' job to separate the **true** talent from the rest of the **rubbish**. And, believe me, there are some doozies in the line-up tonight!'

The headmaster coughed awkwardly.

195

'Err, sorry, your Headmastership,' the professor said, fumbling with a scrap of paper. 'What I meant to say was that every SOS student is *unique* and *special* in their own, um … *unique* and *special* way. We're big on encouraging our students here at SOS, aren't we students?'

There was an awkward **SILENCE**. Somewhere in the distance a cricket chirped. chirp … chirp … chirp …

I don't think it was enrolled at the school.

The headmaster coughed a second time.

'And moving right along,' Professor Porkchop spluttered. 'Why don't we welcome our first act onto the stage? Ladies and gentlesouls, I give you, *Fashion by Deluchio*.'

There were several wolf whistles as the curtains rolled back and a handsome grey wolf swaggered onto the stage, wearing a snazzy new suit from the Uni-Corn Shop. I could see why they were called *wolf* whistles.

196

'Hi, I'm Deluchio da Silva, the **COOLEST** guy on this rat-infested island,' he said in his **SUPERCOOL** wolf voice. 'I'm sure you've all heard of the catwalk. Well, tonight you're going to see a *wolf walk.* That's right, I'm going to walk from one side of the stage to the other, looking totally **COOL,** and you are going to applaud me for my **COOLNESS.** Isn't that right, sugarplum?'

He winked at a random member of the audience who  swooned dramatically and collapsed onto her friends.

'That guy is so **COOL,** it's a crime,' Flick whispered from behind the stage curtain.

'Good for him,' Horace sulked.

'Oh, don't be like that, Horace!' Flick retorted. 'I still think Deluchio is a scumbag – he's just a really **COOL** scumbag.'

'As opposed to us **UN-COOL** scumbags,' Horace said sourly.

'You're no scumbag, Horace,' Flick said.

'You're a rascal.'

'And is that a good thing?' Horace asked.

'I hope so,' Flick replied. 'I'm a rascal, too.'

'Awwww, shucks,' Horace said bashfully. 'That's the *nicest* thing a cat has ever said to me.'

'Group hug!' Benny announced, throwing one arm around Flick and dragging me in with the other. 'Whatever happens tonight, I want you to know that I'm *proud* of you.'

'Thanks, Dad,' Horace squeaked from the centre of the hug. 'I'm proud of me, too.'

When Deluchio had finished acting COOL, and the wolf whistles had finally died down, the judges held up their score cards. It was no surprise to see Legs *Fashion* Lorraine award Deluchio a NINE.

Madam Melody said his performance was pleasing to the eye but lacked any musical merit. She gave him a **SIX**.

Despite the new focus on *encouraging students*, the headmaster gave Deluchio a **TWO**, stating:

THE ENTIRE PERFORMANCE WAS SOFT, WIMPY AND **TOTALLY** UN-PIRATELIKE.

Chips, Chips, Chips!

The next act to take the stage was the Salty Seagulls Community Choir. Led by The Big Chipper, the seagulls flew down from the rafters, where they had been roosting with Sir Squawk-a-lot. They immediately began squabbling over who should stand in the front row.

After much **squawking** and flapping of wings, they eventually found their positions.

'Err, we're the Salty Seagulls Community Choir,' The Big Chipper said nervously. 'We're here to perform a song about our favourite

food. It's called *WE LOVE CHIPS*. I'd like to thank our major sponsor, the Uni-Corn Shop for Fresh (and *deep fried*) Vegetables for supplying us with four thousand buckets of hot chips for tonight's performance. Unfortunately, we ate them all during rehearsals. I'd also like to thank Hook Hand Horace for the line about *kissing my salty lips*. It's a good line. It's very funny.'

Nora poked her head through the open door of her dressing room and hollered:

BUT SEAGULLS DON'T HAVE LIPS. THEY HAVE BEAKS!

AH, GIVE ME A BREAK, NORA. I COULD HARDLY RHYME BEAKS WITH CHIPS, COULD I?

WELL, YOU COULD HAVE USED THE WORD TURNIPS. IT ALMOST RHYMES WITH CHIPS AND IT MAKES FOR A HEALTHY ALTERNATIVE.

'Hey, we're not into turnips!' a one-legged seagull squawked. 'We're into *chips!*'

'HOORAY FOR CHIPS!' chanted the choir. And with that, they burst into song.

♩ Chips, chips, chips.
We love chips! ♪
Hot, salty chips.
Serve them up with dips!

Chips, chips, chips.
We love chips!
Dainty, crispy chips.
Shake your feathered hips!

Chips, chips, chips.
We love chips!
Cannons firing chips
on seagull battleships!

KABOOM!

Chips, chips, chips.
We love chips!
Watch me do backflips
while I'm eating chips!

*Chips, chips,
chips.
We love chips!
Oily, greasy
chips.
We love* 🎵

CHIPS!

No sooner had the final cry of '*CHIPS!*' escaped the seagulls' beaks than a large section of the audience leapt to their feet.

'Oh, look,' Horace said, applauding enthusiastically. 'A standing ovation. It must have been my **kiss my salty lips** line.'

'Not necessarily,' Flick said, pointing to the large crowd gathering in front of Ye Olde Chip Cart. 'I think everyone is off to buy hot chips.'

While the audience queued for over-priced buckets of **oily, greasy chips to put your heart at risk,** the judges expressed their thoughts on the performance.

Madam Melody was impressed with how many words the seagulls could think of that rhymed with *chips*. She gave them an **EIGHT.**

The headmaster was impressed that the bird-brained seagulls could think at all. He also gave them an **EIGHT.**

Legs Lorraine was *not* impressed that the Salty Seagulls had failed to mention her favourite food, *zucchinis,*  which happened to rhyme with *bikinis*. She gave them a **SIX.**

You can't please everyone, I thought as Professor Porkchop introduced the next act.

'Our third victim – I-I mean *contestant* – is Wendi Whiptongue, the *Hilarious Hyena,*' the pig spluttered. 'Please make her welcome, and don't forget to laugh.'

There was plenty of laughter during Wendi's performance (mainly from Wendi), but the jokes were entirely on me.

Take this one for example:

UNCLE MUTTHEW TAKES HIS NEPHEW, MISCHIEF MCSCRUFF, TO SEE A PIRATE MUSICAL.

AS THEY APPROACH THE TICKET BOOTH, MISCHIEF ASKS, 'ARE YOU SURE I'M OLD ENOUGH TO SEE THIS PIRATE MUSICAL, UNCLE? THE SIGN SAYS IT'S RATED ARRR!'

See what I mean?

Not even the headmaster cracked a grin, and he is a huge fan of *ARRR*-rated jokes.

The next joke was even more humiliating.

Mischief McScruff, the scruffiest flea-bag on Shark Tooth Island, goes to the dog-grooming salon for a haircut.

'What'll it be?' the old barber asks.

'Can you make me look like a spunk?' *Mischief asks.*

The barber, who is hard of hearing, takes out his clippers and begins shaving a mohawk into Mischief's head.

'W-what are you doing?'
Mischief splutters.

'I'm making you look like a punk,' *the barber says.*

The pretty poodle sitting in the barber's chair next to Mischief begins to laugh. 'Ha, ha, ha.'

'Do you think this is funny?' Mischief asks.

'Oh, no,' the poodle replies. 'I think it's hair-larious.'

Hair-larious? How is that even funny?

I swear Wendi's third joke came straight out of a Christmas cracker.

What do you call a Sea Dog at the bottom of a deep hole?

ANSWER: Doug.

What do you call a Sea Dog at the bottom of a shallow hole?

ANSWER: Douglas – because he dug less!

DOG DIGS DEEPER

ROCK MARKS THE SPOT

At least Wendi left me alone for her knock, knock joke.

The rest of Wendi's jokes weren't worth repeating, and neither was her score.

As the Talent Quest poster promised, there were some other random SOS acts on the bill. But I doubt you'd want to read about yodelling, shoelace tying, or matchstick model ship building … *yawn*.

And what about Samuel So 'n' Slow? Well, the sleepy sloth drifted onto the stage for his interpretive dance performance with the grace of a swan. Unfortunately, the swan was asleep at the time and moving *SLOWER* than a tortoise with no legs. As for the *interpretive* part of his performance, I can only assume that Samuel was inspired by a giant pink butterfly stuck in a spider's web.

There was no denying that Samuel danced his slowly-beating heart out. But when the backing music started for the *TENTH* time and the audience began snoring loudly, I knew it was curtains for the big guy.

Crunch Time

The night was late, the audience was weary, and the hot chips had finally run out. It was the perfect time to bring out the big guns. Or the **BIG KNIVES** in Chomper's case.

With only three acts remaining until the winner was announced, the Salty Seagulls were in the lead on twenty-two points.

I could tell by the nasty gleam in Chomper's eye that he was ready to knock them off their perch. He also looked ready to **demolish** their nest, **smash** their eggs and **serve** them up with hot chips.

You can tell a lot by looking into a crocodile's eye.

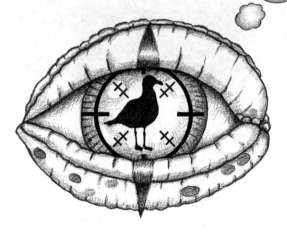

'Psst,' Horace whispered, as Chomper pushed past us onto the stage. 'This looks like *trouble.*'

I followed the direction of Horace's pointing hook. In the shadows at the opposite side of the stage, I saw Wendi and Deluchio creeping up behind Owen Undersea. The little octopus was busy brushing chip crumbs off his top hat. He was fighting a losing battle. For every crumb he removed, another fell from the rafters above him.

Looking up, I saw The Big Chipper munching on chip scraps he had scrounged from the rubbish bin.

Boy, did that guy *LOVE* chips.

While the seagull munched, and Owen cleaned, Chomper called for a volunteer.

IT'S NOTHING DANGEROUS,' he said in a voice that sounded extremely dangerous. 'I just need a volunteer to spin in circles while I throw nasty knives at them.'

Not surprisingly, not a single member of the audience raised a paw.

'Oh look,' Chomper said, pointing in Owen's direction. 'Here is an eager volunteer.'

Before Owen could do anything to stop them, Wendi and Deluchio had grabbed him by the tentacles and were dragging him onto the stage.

'But-but,' he spluttered. 'I didn't, I never –'

'Now, now,' Chomper said. 'We all saw your tentacle raised in the air.'

'I-I was brushing chip crumbs off my hat!' the octopus squeaked. **'HONESTLY!'**

'A likely excuse,' Chomper snorted. 'Now pipe down and let my associates tie you to that spinning wheel while I entertain the crowd with some sword swallowing.'

There was a sudden TH**U**M**P**I**N**G of feet as Nora the Magnificent hopped out of her dressing room.

STOP!
YOU CAN'T
HAVE HIM!
OWEN IS MY
ASSISTANT.

'Too bad,' Chomper said, brushing her away with a wave of his enormous paw. 'The kid's in **my** show now. You can have him when I'm done.'

'But he'll be in pieces!' Nora protested. 'Or even worse, he'll be too traumatised to remember his lines. My entire act will be RUINED!'

'Oh, don't be such a drama queen,' Wendi cackled. 'At least not until it's your turn on stage.'

'Oooh,' Nora fumed. 'This is no joking matter –'

'Students, please,' the headmaster cut in. 'The audience has paid to be entertained, so stop bickering and start entertaining!'

'Aye, Headmaster. With pleasure, Headmaster,' Chomper said. He began removing his longsword from its scabbard.

Nora sulkily retreated into her dressing room, muttering, 'That conniving crocodile planned this from the start …'

While Wendi and Deluchio tied Owen's eight squirming tentacles to the SOS raffle wheel, Chomper entertained the crowd.

First, he stuck the entire blade of his longsword down his throat, receiving a **ROAR** of approval from the headmaster.

OPEN WIDE AND SAY AHH.

It was an impressive trick, but I had seen Chomper stick more than a sword down his throat before.

During the previous term alone, he had swallowed an ironing board, a lamp shade, three oars and a hat stand. He even managed to swallow the kitchen sink. And that was not to mention the library books. Chomper had squeezed in an impressive seventy-two books from the *Cat* shelf of the *Zoology* aisle before Mrs Nibblesworth walked into the library and he was forced to close his mouth. As usual, she accused me of stealing the books and turning them into paper pirate hats. For once, I had talked my way out of trouble, claiming that no self-respecting Sea Dog would wear a paper pirate hat featuring a cat.

FUR

EYES

WHISKERS

CATS, CATS & MORE CATS
All you ever wanted to know

CAT HAT!
UNCOOL!

But back to the talent quest …

Chomper's next trick was to throw the sword high into the air before catching it between his teeth. Using his powerful jaws, he then crunched it into little pieces and swallowed them.

He received an even LOUDER round of applause for his efforts. I had my doubts about the sword. From my angle, the metal blade looked suspiciously like painted wood.

Wendi and Deluchio finished strapping Owen to the raffle wheel and Chomper introduced his final, thrilling stunt.

Owen **squealed!**
The audience **cheered!**
Flick *rolled* her eyes in disgust.

'He could have at least painted over the raffle prizes,' she said. 'I mean, look at them: a *Bouquet of Flowers from Ye Olde School Garden*; a *Private Tuition Lesson with Mrs Nibblesworth*; and *Two-for-One Pies at Pandora's Pie Palace* … Hardly wheel-of-death material.'

Personally, I was more concerned about Owen's safety than a *Lifetime Subscription to Zoology Weekly*.

Chomper continued his explanation. 'Using my superior crocodilian powers, I will throw nasty knives at the Wheel of Death while blindfolded.' He whipped out a large, white handkerchief and swished it through the air.

The audience cheered even **LOUDER!**

Chomper gestured for them to be quiet. 'Yes, yes, I know I'm amazing, but for this

trick to work, I require my assistant to tell me exactly when to throw. Can you do that, Squirmy?'

Owen stopped squirming and let out a pathetic whimper.

'I'll take that as a **yes**,' Chomper said. 'Now, listen up. I will be aiming for the top of the wheel, directly above the axle. Once Owen's tentacles are clear of that mark, he will cry **NOW,** or *Chomper you're amazing* – something like that.'

'What about **STOP?**' Owen ventured. 'I like the word *STOP* …'

Chomper waggled a finger at him. 'No, no, there will be no stopping until every last knife has been thrown. And I have a **lot** of knives.'

Owen turned the colour of curdled milk. And for those of you who don't know your dairy products, curdled milk is off-white, with a hint of **SICKLY YELLOW**.

Chomper wrapped the handkerchief around his eyes.

Chomper's two henchmen gave the wheel an almighty heave, before darting for cover behind the stage curtains.

The enormous crocodile raised his first throwing knife into the air. 'Any time now, Squirmy.'

Owen stared back from the wheel, his octo-eyes *bulging*.

Most of the audience held their breath. Several continued to snore peacefully.

'I'm waiting,' Chomper growled.

Owen hesitated for a moment and then squeaked, **'NOW!'**

The knife rocketed through the air like a ... err, well, like a knife rocketing through the air.

The blade struck the raffle wheel with a shuddering *THUD–D–D.* A huge cheer rose up from the audience. Even the snorers joined in.

Peering closer, I saw the hilt of the

knife protruding from a prize reading, *No Detention in the Dog House for a Month.*

I could sure use that prize, I thought.

'Are you ready for the next nasty knife?' Chomper roared to the crowd.

'**YES!**' the crowd roared back.

'**NO,**' Owen moaned.

Chomper mistook Owen's *no* for a *now* and his second knife was whistling through the air even quicker than his first.

Luckily, the blade struck the raffle wheel's consolation prize: *Extra Salt with Every Bucket of Hot Chips from the SOS Canteen.*

Owen let out a sigh of relief. I made a mental note to discuss the school's healthy food policy with Professor Porkchop – if SOS even had a healthy food policy.

The nasty knives kept coming.

To Chomper's credit, he hit the spaces between Owen's tentacles every time. His shots were **DEAD** accurate. And by that, I mean they were all complete misses.

What Chomper hadn't factored into his grand plan was that, with every spin, Owen was becoming dizzier and dizzier.

Soon his words began to slur, and he struggled to know the right time to yell, **'Naawoo,'** (or whatever was dizzy octopus speak for *now*).

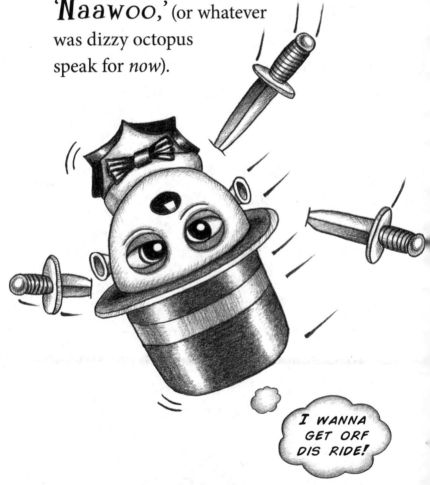

I WANNA GET ORF DIS RIDE!

'We have to do something,' I whispered as the knives edged closer to Owen's tentacles.

'Like what?' Horace said. 'Throw ourselves into the path of a speeding knife blade? Forget it. Owen has **EIGHT** legs. He can afford to lose a **FEW**.'

Flick shot him a look of disapproval.

'I was kidding,' Horace said, raising his hook. 'As a one-pawed Pie Rat I'm allowed to say these things.'

'And as a cat I'm allowed to *eat* you,' Flick replied.

'Point taken,' Horace mumbled.

Horace may have said more, but I wasn't really listening. My attention was focused on the centre of the raffle wheel, my nose *twitching* like mad. Something was wrong. Something I should have noticed earlier.

'Come on,' I hissed, dragging Benny towards the back of the stage. 'I know a way to save that octopus.'

Wheel of Fortune

The SOS raffle wheel consisted of a large wooden wheel with a hole in its centre. The wheel was connected to a tripod by a short axle. A metal pin held the wheel in place. By removing the metal pin, the wheel was free to ROLL away (usually down a steep hill).

LUCKY POINTER THINGY

WHEEL

PIN

AXLE →

TRIPOD

I'm sure there are other scientific points I should mention, but science has never been one of my strong subjects.

As you may have guessed, the metal pin was, at that very moment, in my pocket. My hunch was that one of Chomper's evil henchmen had dropped it while lugging the wheel onto the stage. They either didn't notice it was missing, or they were too lazy to search for it.

Without the pin, the only thing stopping the wheel from spinning off its axle was a little thing called *gravity* (hey, I do know something about science).

Unlike a cart wheel, which was attached **VERTICALLY,** the raffle wheel **LEANED** back on the tripod, keeping it in place. All it would take was a hard shove from behind to send it on its merry way.

I had never been great at **HARD**

233

SHOVING and what MINISCULE muscles I did have were impossible to find under all that scruffy hair. Call me a weakling, but I blame my lack of strength entirely on the closure of the SOS gym.

Luckily, I had Benny to help me.

A diet of bananas should make him ten times stronger than me, I thought.

BANANAS + BENNY = STRENGTH!

I quickly explained my plan to Benny as we reached the back of the stage.

'Bruised bananas!' he exclaimed. 'Are you out of your mind?'

'Possibly,' I admitted. 'But desperate times call for desperate measures. And nasty knives call for even MORE desperate measures.'

'All right, Mischief,' Benny said with a shake of his head. 'But you'd better hope that no one catches us. The punishment for sabotaging a talent quest act is an entire **MONTH** of detention in the Dog House.'

'I'm already in detention for the next three weeks,' I said with a sigh. 'Professor Porkchop caught me turning my science homework into a paper pirate hat. An extra week won't hurt.'

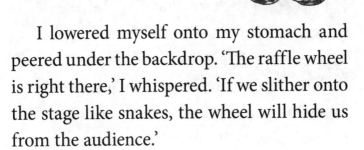

YOU'RE IN THE DOG HOUSE FOR HOMEWORK ABUSE, McSCRUFF!

I lowered myself onto my stomach and peered under the backdrop. 'The raffle wheel is right there,' I whispered. 'If we slither onto the stage like snakes, the wheel will hide us from the audience.'

'And what happens when the wheel starts rolling?' Benny asked in concern.

I turned my head and examined the piles

of old stage props at the back of the stage.

'Perfect,' I said, spotting a rolled-up curtain on the floor. 'Climb in here. We'll blend right in.'

We squirmed inside the dusty curtain and began wriggling onto the stage.

The folds of the curtain made us look more like two **FAT** caterpillars than slithering snakes, though I doubted we would turn into beautiful butterflies for our escape.

I could hear the **ROAR** of the crowd as Chomper's knives continued to pepper the raffle wheel.

'Oh, my precious tentacles,' Owen moaned as the near misses became even nearer misses. 'I can't be a **PIR8TE** with only **SEVEN** legs …'

We increased our pace, hiding in the shadows of the raffle wheel.

'The wheel is just ahead,' I hissed to Benny. 'Get ready to push.'

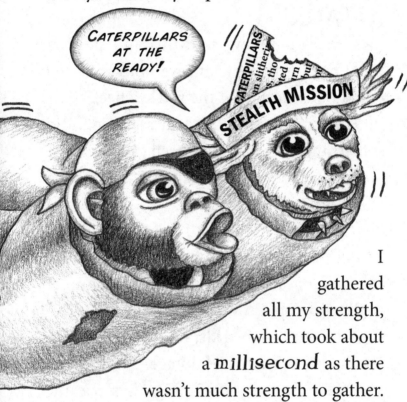

I gathered all my strength, which took about a millisecond as there wasn't much strength to gather. We rose like a two-headed caterpillar behind the raffle wheel. Benny was a pro at this sneaking-up business. I, on the other hand, collided with the tripod and almost fell *FLAT* on my face.

Steadying myself, I gave Benny the pre-arranged signal of, 'CATERPILLARS ATTACK!'

Owen must have heard us and stopped moaning. In that instant we both rammed our shoulders against the raffle wheel.

I heard a small *pop* as my shoulder did something that shoulders aren't supposed to do, followed by an even larger POP as the wheel lurched off the axle.

'Caterpillars down!' I hissed, and the two of us dropped to the deck quicker than caterpillars escaping from hungry seagulls.

Peering up, I saw the spinning wheel hit the wooden floorboards, bounce twice, and then go racing across the stage.

Owen began screaming hysterically. 'Crocodiles and caterpillars are out to kill me! What next? Crazy cockatoos?'

I felt something whiz over my head as the blindfolded crocodile continued to throw his knives in the direction of Owen's voice.

238

Audience members dived under chairs. Townsfolk screamed things I dare not repeat in the pages of a children's book. Oh, all right, I'll repeat what Madam Melody said:

Headmaster von Ironheart simply sat in his seat grinning.

'Soggy dog biscuits! What have we done?' I exclaimed as the wheel reached the front of the stage and launched itself over the edge.

Legs Lorraine let out a startled CROAK and leapt clear as the raffle wheel dropped into the front row, demolishing her chair. Gathering *speed*, it took off down the centre aisle, followed by a stream of knives.

One of Chomper's nasty knives sliced through Owen's ropes, freeing his SIXTH tentacle. Although it may have been his FIFTH tentacle. I'm not an expert when it comes to spinning octopus tentacles.

Anyway, with a tentacle free, Owen began untying himself.

With the spotlight on the runaway raffle wheel, and the Sea Shanty Theatre in chaos, Benny and I crept backstage.

Nora Nibblesworth dashed past us hollering, 'Come back, Owen! I need you for **my** act!'

Despite Nora's pleas, Owen's assistant days were over. The little octopus managed to free himself seconds before the raffle wheel collided with the cart of hot chips, sending salt, sauce and chip oil flying into the air.

'Talk about *fast* food,' Benny whistled.

KERSPLAT!

Owen wasted no time in
DIVING into the lilypond,
where he disappeared beneath
the surface in a shower of bubbles.

Back on the stage, Chomper had finally run out of knives. Hearing the commotion around him, he removed his blindfold to see the theatre in chaos and the Headmaster holding up a score of **NINE**.

'Now that's what I'm talking about!' Chomper chuckled.

The other two judges weren't quite as impressed with Chomper's performance.

Legs Lorraine deducted points for her broken chair and gave him an **EIGHT**. Madam Melody deducted even more points for the hole in her knickers and awarded him a **SEVEN**.

'That still puts me in the lead on twenty-four points,' Chomper boasted to Wendi and Deluchio. 'Now, which one of you nitwits left the *pin* off the axle …?'

Nora the Magnificent

It was only a matter of time before Chomper figured out that a certain scruffy Sea Dog had tampered with the wheel. Wisely, I remained hidden under the curtain.

While the audience straightened their chairs, and pulled knife blades from their knickers, Nora paced around in a RAGE! Her assistant was gone and nothing – not even a sturdy fishing line – was going to coax him out of the lilypond.

Pretty please, Owen. I NEED YOU!

NOPE.

As the drawcard of the event, Nora the Magnificent was expected to **WOW** the audience with her dazzling feats of magnificence – something she couldn't do without a capable assistant.

The three judges met with her behind closed curtains to find a solution. I listened from my cosy caterpillar cave as the headmaster delivered his verdict.

'… you'll simply have to find another assistant, Nora,' he said firmly. 'The school's reputation is at stake, and the show must go on.'

'What about that young Sea Dog from the dog-grooming joke?' Madam Melody suggested. 'I met him yesterday. He was very scruffy, but extremely helpful.'

'He's more of a nuisance if you ask me,' the headmaster muttered.

'And his fashion is atrocious,' Legs Lorraine croaked in her French accent. 'Newspaper

pirate hats are sooo last season.'

'You can't deny he loves the theatre, though,' Madam Melody pointed out. 'Especially those *ARRR-rated* musicals.'

'Oh, all right then,' the headmaster relented. 'The mutt's got the job.' He raised his voice to a booming roar. 'MISCHIEF MCSCRUFF, ON STAGE NOW! You are Nora's new assistant.'

'**Me?**' I said, scrambling out of the curtain and onto the stage in a cloud of dust.

'**Him?**' Nora choked.

COUGH!

'**Aye!**' the headmaster roared. 'You heard what I said. The flea-ridden pooch is your new assistant. Unless you'd prefer a pesky Pie Rat?'

'Hey!' Horace called from the opposite side of the stage.

LEAVE US
PIE RATS
ALONE!

'Fine,' Nora snapped. 'Mischief is hired. But he'd better not botch things up.' She handed me Owen's assistant jacket, which she had salvaged from the lilypond.

'Um, Nora,' I said, studying the soggy jacket closely. 'This has **EIGHT** sleeves.'

'So?' Nora bristled. 'You have **TWO** arms, **TWO** legs, **TWO** ears, **ONE** tail, and **one** nose. That makes **EIGHT**.'

'Err, right,' I said, unable to fault her maths. 'But I might have to make a few adjustments.'

While I fixed my outfit in Nora's dressing room, Nora arranged her props on the stage.

'Where are you, Mischief?' she hissed as Professor Porkchop began his introduction.

'Coming, Nora – I-I mean coming *Nora the Magnificent*,' I replied, scurrying onto the darkened stage.

We stood side by side, facing the closed curtain. The sound of the professor's voice drifted through the thick fabric.

'... this is what you've all been waiting for!'

'So, what exactly does an assistant do?' I whispered.

'An assistant does exactly what I tell them to do,' Nora said. 'No questions asked.'

'But –' I began.

'No questions asked!' she hissed.

The professor continued his introduction,

'... presenting NORA THE MAGNIFICENT!'

The curtains rolled back to reveal a cheering, laughing audience.

The CHEERS were definitely for Nora the Magnificent. The LAUGHS were clearly for my ridiculous octopus' outfit. I had stuffed the spare sleeves with empty chip buckets and used leftover chips for fingers.

Nora, seeing my outfit for the first time in the spotlight, suddenly looked horrified.

'What the Tasmanian devil are you thinking?' she fumed.

I felt like singing *chips, chips, chips, good to mend outfits*. But I simply shrugged instead. There was no point getting off to a bad start.

Nora walked over to a small table.

'For my first magnificent trick,' she announced to the audience, 'I will ask my **UNFASHIONABLE** assistant to pick a card from this deck.'

She spread the playing cards face-down on the table and I selected one at random.

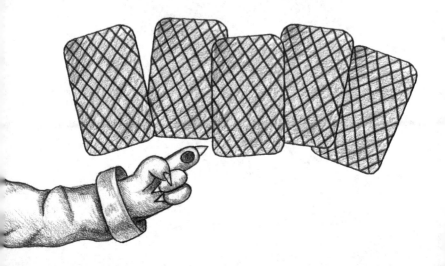

'Please look at your card,' she instructed.

As I went to turn the card over, I was distracted by a shadowy, green figure skulking past a bucket of carrots on the side of the stage.

Chomper O'Many, I thought. *What's he up to?*

'Now, please show your card to the audience,' Nora continued. 'But do not show it to me.'

With thoughts of Chomper still on my mind, I held the card up for the crowd to see. There was a soft murmur as they took in the design.

WHISPER ...
WHISPER ...

'Now, please return the card to the deck,' Nora said.

I placed the card on the top of the deck and Nora worked her magic. She cut the deck several times and did some fancy card shuffling, before pulling out a card at random and holding it up for all to see.

'Is **THIS YOUR CARD?**' she asked dramatically.

I stared at the design. It was the **THREE** of **HEARTS.** I vaguely recalled seeing a heart (or possibly a diamond) on my card, but I had been too distracted by Chomper to pay much attention to the number.

'Um …' I said, tapping my nose with a chip finger. 'Can I have a multiple choice?'

The audience burst out laughing.

Nora stamped her foot in frustration and hurled the cards across the stage.

'How hard is it to remember **ONE** stupid card?' she snapped.

Extremely hard when there's a saltwater crocodile on the prowl, I thought.

Nora led me over to a wooden coffin. 'For my next trick, I will saw my **FORGETFUL** assistant in half, and then put him back together again.'

The audience cheered ecstatically. This was the kind of trick they had paid to see.

Nora opened the lid of the coffin and picked up a large, shiny saw.

'Please climb in,' she instructed. 'And place your head and your feet through the holes at either end.'

SOMETHING DOESN'T FEEL RIGHT ...

What the audience couldn't see from their seats was that the coffin had been custom built for the act. Instead of sticking my legs right through the coffin, I tucked them up around my chest.

As I climbed inside, Nora pulled a secret lever and a set of fake feet popped out the other end.

'Ta-daaa!' Nora cried.

The audience **ROARED** with laughter.

HA, HA, HA!

Nora's face soured.

Peering down, I saw the cause of her distress. The fake feet she had constructed belonged to an octopus, not a dog. Four slimy tentacles would have looked fine if her former assistant, Owen, was in the coffin, but not a shaggy mutt.

'Stupid stage props!' Nora snorted, cutting through the fake octopus tentacles with one frustrated swing of her saw.

The audience laughed even *LOUDER*.

Nora dragged me out of the coffin and pointed to the bucket of carrots.

'Go stand over there,' she ordered. 'And wait for my instructions.'

I trudged over to the bucket, relieved to see that Chomper was nowhere in sight.

Nora hopped onto the small table.

'Ladies and gentlemen,' she announced, 'I will now juggle **SIX** carrots while balancing an Easter egg on my head.'

She removed a brightly-coloured Easter egg from a box of props and placed it on her forehead.
'On my command, my **INFURIATING** assistant will throw me one carrot at a time until a total of six carrots are being juggled.'

Nora turned to face me, the Easter egg still balanced on her forehead. 'Are you ready, assistant Mischief?'

'Aye, Nora the Magnificent,' I said picking up the first carrot.

'Then let me have it!' she declared.

I threw her the **FIRST** carrot, quickly followed by the **SECOND** and the **THIRD**. Miss Sparkle must have selected the carrots by hand as they were all the same length and weight.

On Nora's command, the **FOURTH** and the **FIFTH** carrot were added to the routine.

The pointy orange vegetables began to fly higher and higher.

I reached into the bucket for the **SIXTH** and final carrot. It felt strangely *light* in my paw. I looked down to see that it was half the length of the other carrots. All that remained of its pointy end was a jagged line of teeth marks.

'Chomper!' I gasped. 'Chomper's been *CHOMPING* again!'

CRUNCH, CRASH, BOOM!

I had barely picked up the sabotaged carrot, when I heard my name being called.

'Mischief. I need that sixth carrot.'

'But Nora –' I spluttered.

'The sixth carrot, **NOW!**' Nora snapped.

What choice did I have? I could hardly deny a bunny of her carrots.

I tossed the half-eaten carrot through the air, praying the pointy end was just there for show.

It *wasn't*. The pointy end was the part Nora tried to catch.

With a startled gasp, the bunny's fingers clamped around thin air.

The carrot continued its course, striking Nora in the centre of her nose.

The Easter egg went spinning across the stage, where it was immediately set upon by two Salty Seagulls.

Nora the Magnificent took a magnificent dive backwards, plunging head-first into the open coffin. The carrots rained down on her like tenpins.

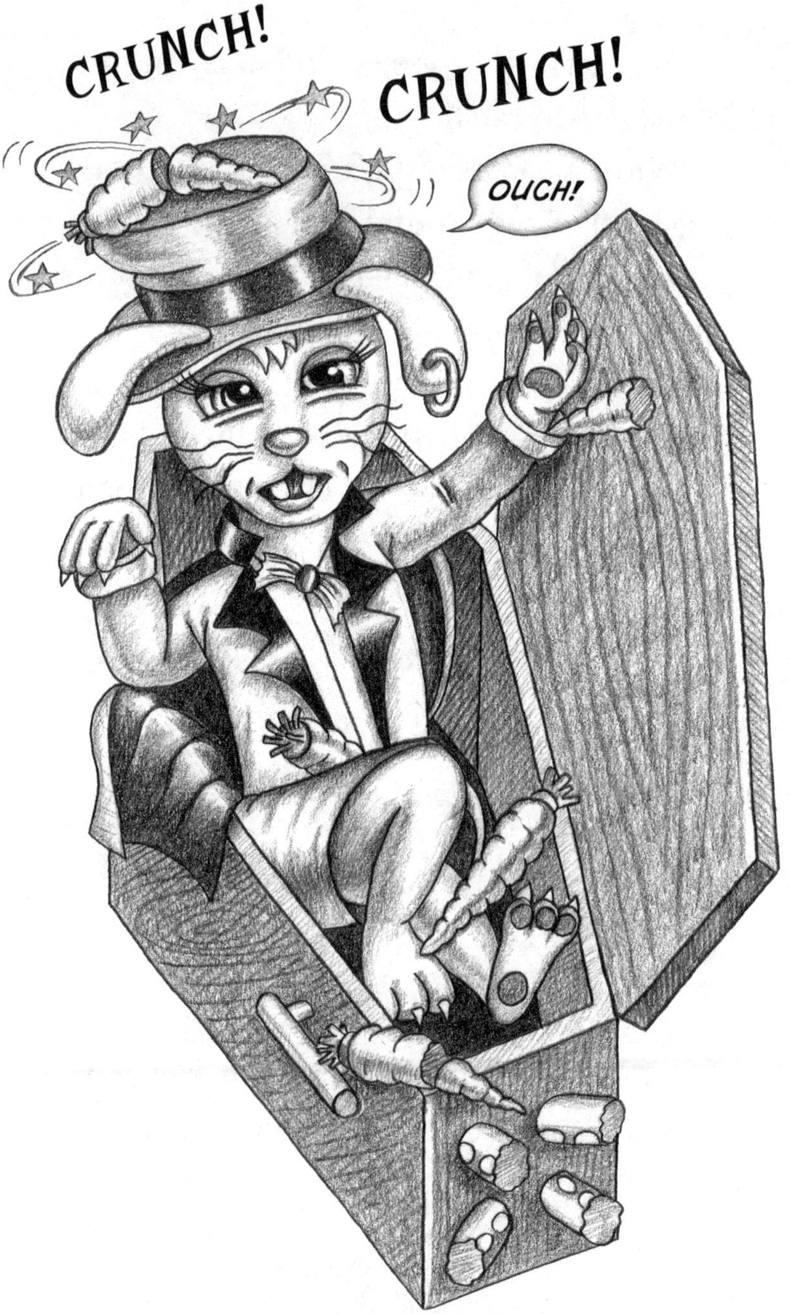
CRUNCH!
CRUNCH!
OUCH!

You could not have scripted a funnier routine. The entire theatre erupted into laughter.

Nora clambered out of the coffin, red-eyed and delirious. Looking like a character from a Halloween musical, she let out a zombie-like **GROAN**, then waved me towards an enormous magician's hat at the back of the stage.

'Rabbit in a hat,' she moaned. 'Have to finish with rabbit in a hat …'

The hat, I realised, was not a hat at all, but an enormous hat-shaped cannon.

It was aimed at a safety net on the opposite side of the stage. A small barrel of gunpowder stood beside it.

'Prepare the hat for lift off ...' Nora continued in the same slurred voice.

Picking up the barrel, I climbed up a short ladder. 'How much gunpowder should I add?' I asked.

'The agreed amount,' Nora said, staggering closer.

I hadn't agreed to *any* amount, so I followed the basic rule of:

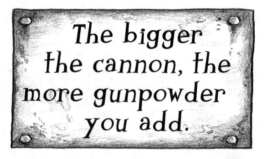

The bigger
the cannon, the
more gunpowder
you add.

Nora's cannon was extremely **BIG**, so I tipped in the *entire* barrel of gunpowder.

'That should do the trick,' I said, dusting off my paws.

I helped Nora up the ladder and into the barrel of the cannon where she put on a coconut-shell safety helmet. In hindsight she should have worn the helmet during her previous routine, but carrot juggling had never been considered a dangerous sport.

Despite Nora's dizziness, she insisted we finish her act with, '*ONE BIG MAGNIFICENT BANG!*'

'Light her up, Owen!' she cried with unfocused eyes. 'I'm going on a trip to the moon …'

Although my name wasn't Owen, and a trip to the moon sounded scientifically doubtful, I followed her instructions and lit the fuse.

The audience counted down as the sparking fuse hissed towards the cannon barrel.

FIVE! FOUR! THREE! TWO! ONE! BLAST OFF!

There was a huge **KABOOM** as the cannon roared to life. Flames and smoke exploded around me like an erupting volcano.

TO THE SAFETY NET AND BEYOND!

From the moment Nora's body blasted out of the barrel, I knew I should have gone *easy* on the gunpowder.

Instead of following a gentle arc into the safety net, Nora rocketed off the stage, over the audience, through the fig tree and into the lilypond. She hit the water with an almighty **SPLASH,** missing the statue of Blacktail the Bold by millimetres and creating a tidal wave so **BIG** that it reached Legs Lorraine in the front row.

The bikini-clad frog leapt joyfully out of her broken chair, declaring, 'A midnight swim is just what I needed!'

The cold water of the lilypond seemed to sh^{a}ke Nora out of her stupor. She turned to Owen, still hiding in the water and yelled, 'This is all your fault, Owen! Next time I'm

hiring a RELIABLE assistant!'

I just stood there, a smoking match in my paw, wondering what *two* barrels of gunpowder could achieve.

Maybe a trip to the moon was possible ...

As disastrous as Nora's act had been, the judges thoroughly loved it.

I KNEW THERE WAS A REASON I WORE THIS!

Madam Melody said she hadn't laughed so much since PIE FACE THE MUSICAL came to town. Headmaster von Ironheart vowed to add the sport of bunny cannonballing to the SOS athletics carnival.

And Legs Lorraine was simply pleased that she could put her string bikini to good use.

It was no surprise to see the judges award Nora the Magnificent with three straight nines.

And for those of you who don't know your nine times tables:

$$3 \times 9 = 27.$$

'A score like that is going to be hard to beat,' Flick said as we prepared the stage for our Sea Shanty Gangster act.

'True,' Horace said. 'But a win for Nora is a win for Mischief. He totally ROCKED that stage!'

Flick picked up a splinter of coffin wood. 'Rocked or **WRECKED?**' she asked.

'It wasn't intentional,' I confessed, removing my eight-sleeved assistant's jacket. 'And that carrot catastrophe was totally Chomper's fault.'

Flick began hanging a line of white bed sheets across the back of the stage. 'Let's just hope Chomper leaves *our* act alone.'

'I think Chomper has retired for the evening,' Horace said, peering through the gap in the front curtain. 'He's sitting in the back row with Wendi and Deluchio looking mighty annoyed.'

FOILED AGAIN!

'I don't blame him,' I said. 'All those failed attempts to sabotage Nora's act handed her the lead. As my Uncle Mutthew would say, *crime never pays.*'

'Unless you're a successful pirate,' Horace argued. 'And then it pays handsomely.'

'Err … guys,' Flick interrupted. 'Has anyone seen Benny? We're due to start any minute and he seems to have vanished.'

I looked around in horror. 'You don't think Chomper could have –?'

'Relax,' Horace said. 'Benny is in Nora's dressing room, trying on her jewellery.'

'He's doing **WHAT?**' Flick gasped.

'Don't worry, it's nothing creepy,' Horace

274

said. 'He just wanted some more gangster bling. I'll go and fetch him if you like.'

While Horace went to fetch Benny from the dressing room, Flick and Sir Squawk-a-lot made some last-minute adjustments to the stage props.

I was left alone with my panpipe.

There had been so much drama that evening that I hadn't had time to think about our act. All night I had played the fool, but it was finally my chance to do something noteworthy (and by that, I mean playing *notes* that were *worthy* of applause). Panpiping wasn't exactly rocket science, but, for an accident-prone mutt like me, it was a big ask.

Most of all, I didn't want to let my friends down. Benny was **GIFTED,** Flick was **ARTISTIC,** and Horace made people **LAUGH.** Even Sir Squawk-a-lot was talented in his own **ABSURD** way. I just seemed to botch things up.

Not tonight, I told myself. *Tonight, you are going to* **SHINE.** I didn't mean *literally* **SHINE** – that was Flick's job. She was our lighting technician. My job was to hide in the shadows and scare the living daylights out of everyone. But as much as a spooky-sounding panpiper could **SHINE,** I was going to **SHINE.**

'We're all set,' Flick said. She took her place behind the white sheets with a lantern, a pile of dried seaweed and some six-day-old leftovers from the school canteen.

WHAT A STENCH!

Sir Squawk-a-lot perched above her, holding the strings of a strange, hairy puppet.

Horace joined me backstage. His drumstick attachment was fastened to his stump. A small drum and pile of broken shells lay at his feet.

'Are you ready to give the audience some **REAL** entertainment?' he asked with a grin.

PREPARE FOR A SCARE!

DUM DUM

DUMM!

The Legend Revealed

Hiccupping loudly, Professor Porkchop took to the stage to introduce the final act.

'The *Sea Shanty Gangster Rap* has been reserved until last so that parents of young children can leave before the swearing and cursing begins. However, Benny Banana Peel assures me that tonight's performance contains **NO** rude words, **NO** rude hand gestures and **NO** shaking hips.'

HIC!

'Shake your feathered hips! It's a chip eclipse!' The Big Chipper squawked from the rafters.

The professor shook his trotter at the seagull. 'Hey, that's enough from you! You've had your shot at stardom. Now go and lay an egg, or something.'

Ignoring the hip-shaking seagull, Professor Porkchop returned his attention to the audience. 'Without further interruption, I give you the **SEA SHANTY GANGSTER RAPPER!'**

A few animals clapped, but most of them just yawned and checked their pocket watches. The curtains opened to reveal a backdrop of white bedsheets. As far as set designs went, it was hardly a masterpiece.

Benny strolled onto the stage, wearing every piece of gangster bling he owned (plus every piece that Nora owned). He looked like he had just robbed a jewellery store.

'YO, WAZZUUUP?' he said in his best gangster voice.

'The sky,' shouted The Big Chipper. 'And the moon, and the stars. And sometimes seagulls are up, but most of the time we're down in the rubbish bins scrounging –

chips, chips, chips,
we love chips ...'

Benny waited until the seagull had finished his verse before continuing.

'We had planned to perform a jolly little shanty about the history of Shark Tooth Island,' he explained. 'But, as midnight approaches, we thought it would be more fitting to give you something SPINE-TINGLING. Ladies and gentlemen, on this very stage, the mystery of the Hungry Hairy Sea Monster is about to be revealed.'

On cue the spotlights faded, and the theatre was plunged into eerie darkness.

The entire audience sat up in their chairs. All except Legs Lorraine, whose broken chair had been washed away in the tidal wave.

Even The Big Chipper stopped heckling and paid attention.

'Now, I'm sure there are some sceptics out there,' Benny said. 'And for those of you who need to see to believe, we have invited a *special guest* along ...'

A circle of pale light appeared on the sheets behind Benny. It was like moonlight shining through mist.

At the same time, a strange seaweed-scented smoke began drifting across the stage.

Benny paused for dramatic effect, then began to rap.

It's hungry and
it's HAIRY,

and positively
SCARY.
It pays to be
quite WARY

on any
moonlit night.

The audience began to mutter nervously.

'They ain't seen nothin' yet!' Horace whispered.

Benny commenced the second verse and Horace began his drumming. He started with a soft, plodding rhythm, *dum, dum, dum,* but increased his pace as the verses went on. With every **THUMP** of the drum came the **CRUNCH** of breaking shells.

It's footsteps
sound like THUNDER,

a terrifying
WONDER.
You might just
hear it LUMBER

across the
Bog tonight.

THUMP!

It smells like
mouldy MUESLI,

and sewage-
flavoured SUSHI,
and some strange
dish, TABOULI,

and fruit that's
over-ripe.

The stench of burning seaweed and rotten leftovers was **DISGUSTING**, to say the least.

But it was during the next verse that the real drama began. Surrounded by moonlight, a strange, hairy shadow appeared on the back of the bedsheets.

It was nothing more than Sir Squawk-a-lot's puppet – a collection of cat hair and seaweed stuck to an old cushion with sticks for legs and spiral shells for horns – but the way it lumbered forward in time with the drumming, was enough to **RATTLE** even the hardest of scoundrels.

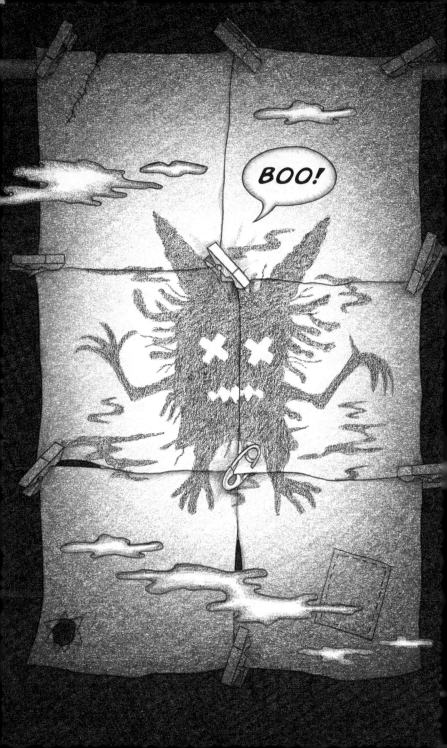

Beware the hungry
MONSTER.

I swear it's
no IMPOSTER!
And mind it does
not CHOMP YA,

or give you one
big fright!

And just when the audience thought things couldn't get any more terrifying, I raised the panpipe to my lips and began to play.

I played with soul, I played with passion, but mostly I played with **BIG, GULPING** breaths.

The haunting tune of the panpipes echoed across the stage. It drifted down the aisles. Like wind on an arctic sea, it sent *icy* chills down the spines of all who heard it.

Hello, Olivia. I tried to make the pictures funny (and a bit scary), but most are just plain silly! Dad

It was **INESCAPABLE**.

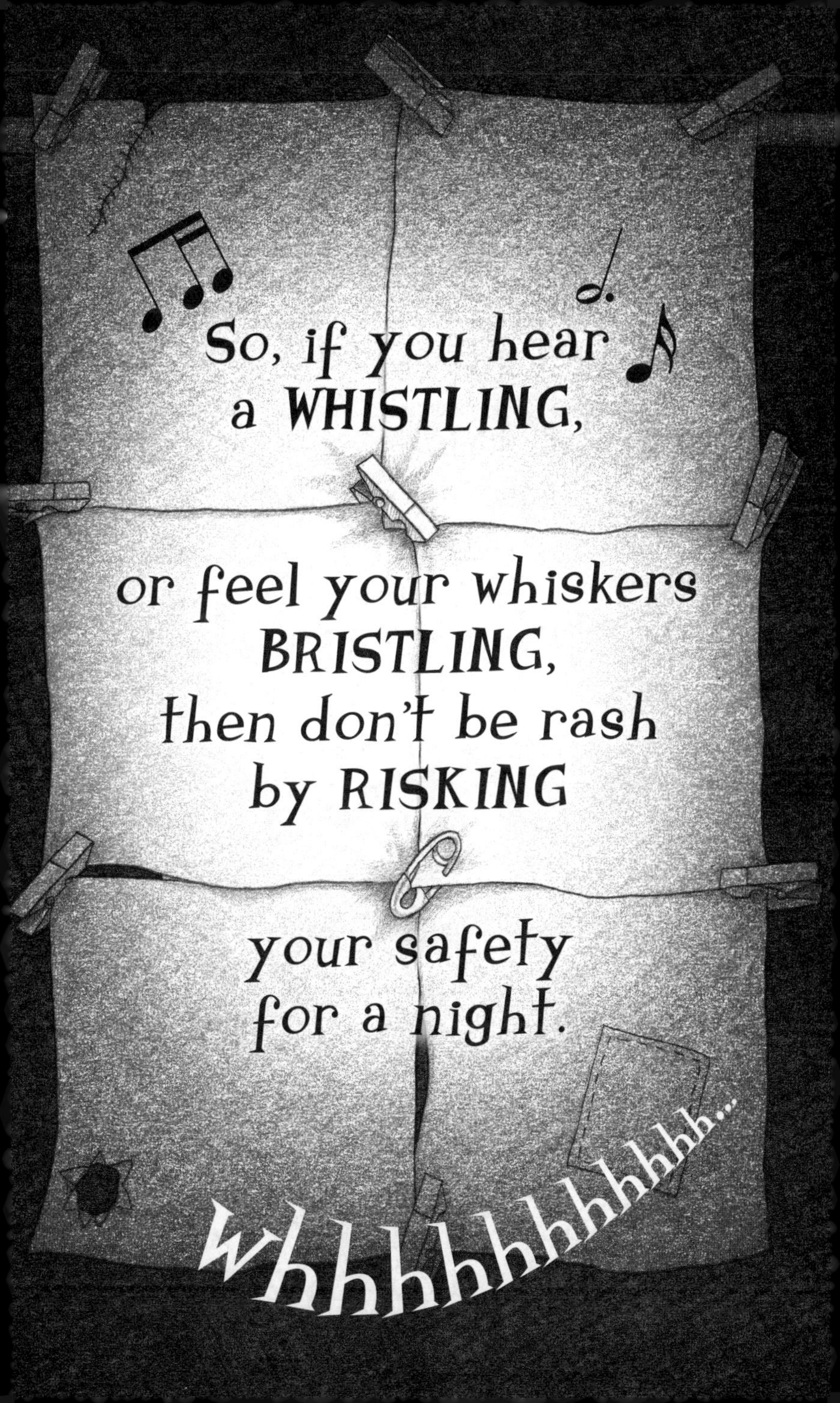

So, if you hear
a WHISTLING,

or feel your whiskers
BRISTLING,
then don't be rash
by RISKING

your safety
for a night.

whhhhhhhhh...

It was at this point, when the **whistling** and the **drumming** were building to a crescendo, that the shadow of the monster grew *LARGER*

and **LARGER**

and **LARGER**

until it filled the entire backdrop.

Benny rapped the final verse like the creature was about to swallow him whole (or peel him like a banana).

The truth could
not be CLEARER.

I see it drawing
NEARER.
I'm petrified with
FEAR, AHHH!

Quick! Run away!
Take flight!

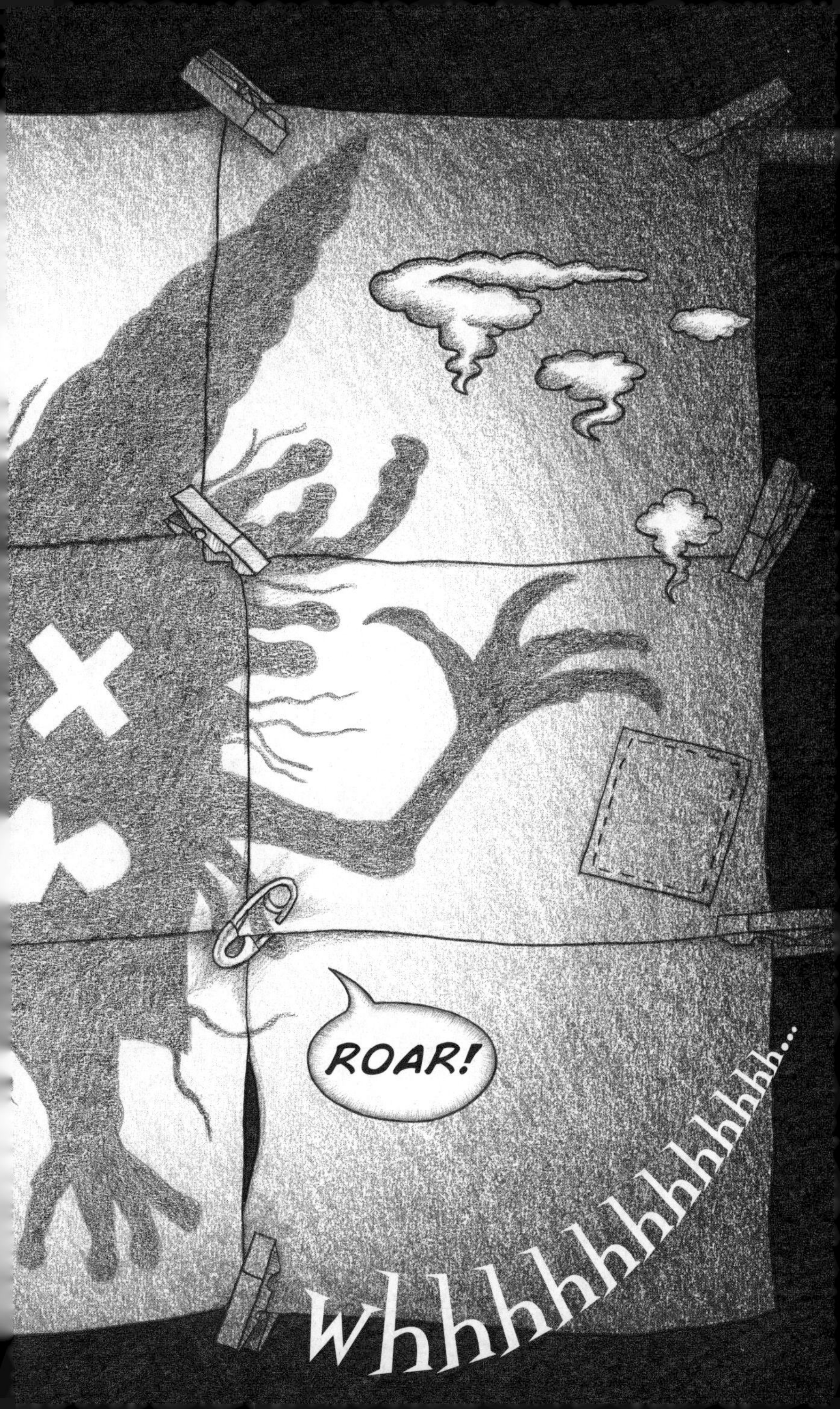
ROAR!
whhhhhhhhhhhh...

Winners and Whingers

Benny's warning was all the encouragement the audience needed. Mothers **SCREAMED,** fathers **SCREAMED** even louder, and there wasn't a single student who didn't wet their pants, or howl like a hyena – and I'm not just talking about Wendi Whiptongue.

Chairs were overturned, handbags were sent *flying,* and empty chip buckets were trampled into the mud in the rush to escape.

The school hadn't seen such panic since a plague of killer wasps swept over the island.

'**Shiver me stampedes!**' Horace exclaimed. 'I didn't expect our performance to be **THAT** convincing.'

When the chaos had finally died down and the smoke had cleared, we joined Benny on stage to take our bows. A shadowy sentence appeared on the sheets behind us.

SOME
MYSTERIES

AREN'T MEANT
TO BE

REVEALED ...

WHAT HAPPENS AT THE TALENT QUEST, STAYS AT THE TALENT QUEST ...

'At least we kept our promise to the Hungry Hairy Sea Monster,' Flick whispered as we bowed low. 'If the townsfolk didn't believe in him *before* our performance, they certainly do *now*.'

We received a small round of applause from the front row, but there was no chance of an encore. The theatre was practically deserted. Even Chomper had fled the scene, yelling, 'I'm too young to be a *CROCODILE KEBAB!*'

I spotted Nora Nibblesworth in the lilypond, hiding behind the statue of Blacktail the Bold. Blacktail was wearing a strange new octopus-shaped hat.

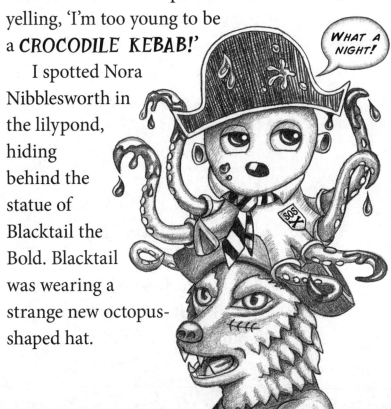

WHAT A NIGHT!

Only the three judges remained. And it wasn't by choice. They had sworn an oath to watch every performance.

'W-w-well,' Madam Melody trembled. 'That was certainly a dramatic way to end the evening. And oh, what a HAUNTING tune. So much emotion.'

I felt my cheeks blushing. It wasn't every day I received a compliment for frightening half the island away.

'And that monster is one stylish beast,' Legs Lorraine croaked, wiping mud off her yellow bikini. 'Long hair is this season's HOT NEW TREND.'

'So, you liked our performance?' Benny said in surprise.

'Not in a laugh-out-loud kind of way,' Madam Melody admitted. 'But when it comes to sheer TERROR, I'd say it was a ten-out-of-ten performance.'

'Bananarrific!' Benny hooted, fist pumping the air. 'The first TEN of the night.'

'I was tossing up between a nine and a ten,' Legs Lorraine admitted. 'But my nine scorecard was trampled into the mud, so I guess it's a *TEN* from me, too.'

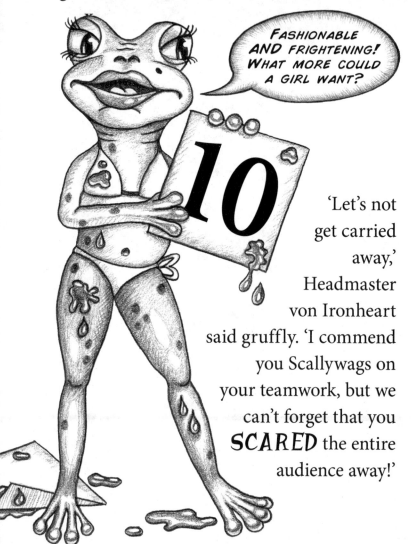

FASHIONABLE *AND FRIGHTENING!* WHAT MORE COULD A GIRL WANT?

'Let's not get carried away,' Headmaster von Ironheart said gruffly. 'I commend you Scallywags on your teamwork, but we can't forget that you **SCARED** the entire audience away!'

'That's a bit harsh,' Horace protested. 'I'd say we *gently encouraged them to leave.*'

'Regardless of how much **ENCOURAGING** you gave them, they are no longer with us,' the headmaster said. He gestured to the empty chairs lying in pieces on the ground. 'I had planned to promote the SOS pie drive at the end of the concert, but with all our potential customers gone, we'll be lucky to sell a **DOZEN** pies.'

'Oooh, sign me up for **TWO DOZEN** piping-hot apple pies!' Horace exclaimed excitedly.

'And I'll take **THREE DOZEN,**' Madam Melody chimed in.

'And what about the other **THREE-HUNDRED-AND-SOMETHING-DOZEN** pies?' the headmaster asked.

'I know a sea monster with a **big** appetite,' I offered. 'He's not exactly rolling in money, but you might get some missing library books back.'

Headmaster von Ironheart shook his grizzly head. 'I'm sorry, but I'll still have to deduct points for causing a stampede and damaging school property. It will take Old Fetch an entire term to repair those chairs.'

I felt my tail sagging. My dreams were about to be *shattered* by a pile of *shattered* furniture. *Just my luck.*

The headmaster held up his score card.

I blinked several times, trying to make out the number in the dim light.

At first, I thought it was a **ONE.** But then I realised it was a **SEVEN.**

'A *seven?*' Horace said in confusion. 'A seven is, err …' He scratched his head. 'Hey, Flick, is seven a *good* score or a *bad* score? I'm terrible at maths this late at night.'

Flick, who was good at maths at any time of the day or night, did some quick calculations.

$$10 + 10 + 7 = 27$$

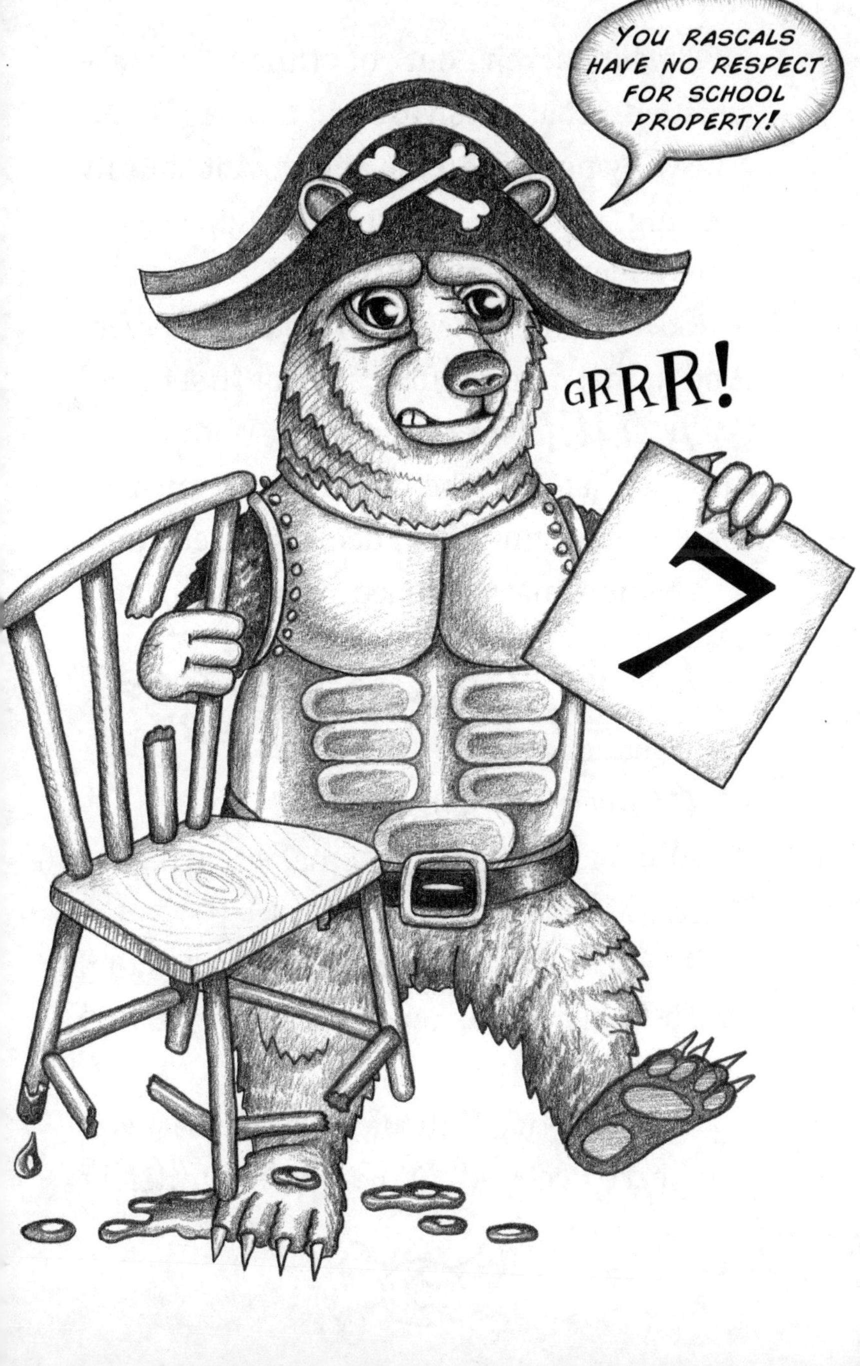
YOU RASCALS HAVE NO RESPECT FOR SCHOOL PROPERTY!
GRRR!
7

'Twenty-seven out of thirty,' Horace whistled. 'That doesn't sound too bad.'

Benny pointed to the angry white bunny hopping towards the stage. 'Didn't Nora score twenty-seven points?'

'So she did!' the headmaster chuckled. 'And in that case, we have a tie for first place.'

'**A TIE!**' Nora exclaimed. 'With them? But-but that can't be right! There must be some kind of mistake. I demand a recount!'

The headmaster sighed. 'Very well …'

10+10+7 =27   AND   9+9+9 =27

'Do my fellow judges agree?'

'Oui,' Legs Lorraine croaked, which I think was French for **yes**.

'La, la, la, la, la,' Madam Melody sang, which I believe was opera speak for **I also agree.**

'It is official then,' Headmaster von Ironheart declared. 'Nora the Magnificent

and the Sea Shanty Gangster Rapper will share this year's honours as joint-winners of the Shark Tooth Talent Quest!'

'But this is an **OUTRAGE!**' Nora exploded. 'It's the disaster of the decade. It's the scandal of the century! A *TIE* with *Bruised* Banana Peel and Mischief *McFailure* is even worse than coming **SECOND.** Nora the Magnificent will be ruined!'

'Now, now, Nora,' the headmaster said. 'You will still have your name engraved on the trophy – just in very SMALL letters.'

'Small letters!' Nora fumed. 'But-but …'

'And we may have to leave off the *Magnificent* bit,' Madam Melody added. 'There are a lot of words to squeeze in.'

'Oooooooo, rotten carrots!' Nora cursed. 'This is the **WORST** night ever!'

And with that, she threw her magnificent hat into the mud and stamped on it.

'Someone is certainly a sore loser,' Horace said as Nora stormed off into the night.

'More like a sore *winner*,' Flick muttered.

'All right, you lot,' the headmaster said with a yawn. 'You might be the new Shark Tooth Talent Quest champions, but this mess won't clean itself up. Find a mop and start mopping.'

'So much for a victory celebration,' Horace groaned.

'Look on the bright side,' I said, as the judges began walking away. 'The headmaster would usually give us an entire **MONTH** of detention for this kind of prank.'

Headmaster von Ironheart turned back to face us with a mirthless grin. 'Oh, I forgot to mention, you have **TWO MONTHS'** detention for destroying school property.'

'Rotten pies to double detention!' Horace moped.

'At least it will give us plenty of time to compose next year's winning performance,' Benny said excitedly. 'I can see it now ...

THE CURSE OF THE DREADED SEA CUCUMBER!'